PATIENCE A

(Ha...

have Read

She'll get no favours from me, vows Dr
Angus Pritchard when he's asked to pull
strings for Nurse Patience Rainer, who's
just started her training at his hospital.
What he doesn't know is that Patience
hates favouritism as much as he does—
and when he finds out, Angus's resolve
seems to melt . . .

Books you will enjoy
in our Doctor Nurse series:

PATIENCE
AND
DR PRITCHARD

BY

LILIAN DARCY

MILLS & BOON LIMITED
15–16 BROOK'S MEWS
LONDON W1A 1DR

First published in Great Britain 1985
by Mills & Boon Limited

© Lilian Darcy 1985

Australian copyright 1985
Philippine copyright 1985

ISBN 0 263 75052 3

Set in 10 on 12 pt Linotron Times
03–0585–54,500

Photoset by Rowland Phototypesetting Ltd
Bury St Edmunds, Suffolk
Made and printed in Great Britain by
Richard Clay (The Chaucer Press) Ltd
Bungay, Suffolk

CHAPTER ONE

Dr Angus Pritchard turned carefully into the rather overgrown driveway of the comfortably proportioned old house that was the home of his godfather. His adequate but by no means flashy little car only narrowly missed one of the white painted gate-posts which had been almost concealed by a leafy section of shrubbery.

Poor old Rover! he thought. It wasn't a recent model and didn't exactly have the smallest turning circle in the world. When he bought himself the long-promised Jaguar, though, things would be different. Driving would become a pleasure then, and he would be able to take the sporty model all over the countryside just for the sheer pleasure of sitting at the wheel. That would have to wait until he got his fellowship, though—not long, he hoped.

The chestnut-haired surgeon recalled his thoughts to the present abruptly. At thirty-two, a successful and still rising doctor may legitimately have his unfulfilled dreams, but there are few times when it is proper for him to indulge in thinking of them. The driveway had terminated in an open gravelled rectangle beside the house, and Gilbert Rainer had emerged from the front door and was standing nearby, waiting to greet his visitor.

Angus climbed out of the car, glad to be able to stretch his athletic legs, although the drive from the hospital had taken only just over an hour.

'Good morning, Uncle . . . er, Uncle Gilbert!' Angus

reached out and shook the older man's hand heartily, although he was feeling a little awkward.

'Good morning, Angus. How are you?'

'Very well, thank you. And you?'

'Nothing to complain about . . . And by the way, it's probably time we stopped this Uncle Gilbert business. First names will do from now on, and that goes for Jean too.'

'Oh, yes, all right then, thank you.'

Gilbert Rainer turned and led the way inside while Angus attempted to recover from what had been a rather strained greeting. He had sensed that the other man had been going through exactly the same thought processes as himself in a vain attempt to recollect how long it actually was since they had seen each other. It must be several years, at least, and Dr Pritchard knew that undoubtedly a few more would have been allowed to elapse before they had met again if it had not been for the fact that the Rainers had a favour to ask of him.

'Something to drink?' Gilbert Rainer said, ushering him into a sunny, family-style sitting-room.

'Yes, that would be nice. It's rather warm out today,' the young surgeon replied politely.

'Something long and cool then?'

'Perfect!'

The older man left the room to prepare the drinks and Angus thought again—and with his usual vague annoyance—of the favour that had been asked of him. His godfather had telephoned out of the blue two weeks ago to make the suggestion, and Angus had not been able to refuse. After all, it was a relatively small thing. It seemed that the Rainers' eldest daughter Patti—whom he dimly remembered as a plump, giggle-prone and freckly little girl—was about to take up nursing at the Sir

Richard Gregory Memorial Hospital, and Uncle Gilbert had asked if it would be possible for Angus to introduce the girl to one or two senior members of the nursing and training staff.

So here he was, about to undergo a large family lunch before driving his protégée up to the outer London suburb where Ricky's, as the hospital was irreverently nicknamed by the staff, was situated.

Quite simply, what the whole thing amounted to, of course, was that little Miss Rainer wanted to have her path made smooth for her at the hospital, and thought that her acquaintance with Dr Angus Pritchard would achieve just that.

It was the kind of thing he despised. If Patti Rainer was a good nurse she would quickly earn the favourable opinion of anyone who mattered, and if she was not, no introduction from a surgeon, no matter how gifted, would get her anywhere. All student nurses were extremely well cared for at the hospital, and any homesickness or loneliness that Patti faced would be nothing more than what dozens of other girls went through.

He felt that the sort of advantage she so obviously desired was simply not fair, and he thought he could picture fairly accurately what the plump little girl in his memory must have become—a rather shallow and grasping person, and probably very naive into the bargain. Apparently she had been working as a stable-hand since leaving school. Dr Pritchard thought he could picture that fairly clearly too. She would have had images of some sort of glamorous life among the hunting set, and when reality had paled in comparison, she had invented a new fantasy about the world of medicine. No doubt it included close relationships with handsome doctors and soothing the fevered brows of millionaire patients. Giggling Patti was on the look-out for a boy-friend . . .

'But I mustn't get carried away,' Dr Pritchard thought, as his host returned with two long glasses of lager.

Uncle Gilbert—or plain Gilbert, as Angus must remember to call him now—had been very good in the past. In that painful period after the death of Angus' father, he had provided both financial and emotional support, and if they had gradually drifted apart over the past ten years, it was no one's fault. Gilbert and Jean Rainer were very good people.

It did make him angry, though, when he loved the medical profession so much, to think of someone entering it for what must be such misguided and unattractive reasons.

Patience Rainer, the object of all these somewhat unflattering thoughts and musings, was unaware that Dr Pritchard had even arrived. She was thinking about him, though, as she wandered around the most distant corner of the extensive vegetable garden, picking salad ingredients for her mother. In fact, she was hoping quite desperately that he would not turn up for lunch at all. Perhaps an emergency operation would detain him . . .

'I'll never forgive Mother for insisting on all this,' she said to herself with a fierce little frown as she viciously twisted the head of a lettuce from the single root which anchored it in the soil. 'Dr Pritchard is probably a pompous creep of a man and all the other student nurses will hate me just because I know him.'

The herbs and vegetables were all picked now and Mrs Rainer would be waiting for them, but Patti could not bring herself to go back into the house just yet. That would signal the moment when she would have to change into the clothes she would wear for the drive to the hospital, and now that it was time to take this first step into the world of nursing, she was not at all sure that she wanted to do it.

Oh, it was not that she had doubts about herself as a nurse—it was just this awful idea of her mother's to have Dr Pritchard introduce her. Because it had been Mrs Rainer's idea, not Patti's, as Angus had mistakenly assumed.

At twenty, Patience Rainer had learnt a little about the world, and she had instinctively and rightly guessed that no one at the hospital would respect, admire, like or notice her any the more for her having been presented by one of the select band of hospital surgeons. But her attempts to talk her mother out of the idea had been in vain. It was not that Jean Rainer was a snob or a social climber, nor that she was unintelligent, but she had forgotten what it was like to be twenty years old and about to plunge into a new and very large environment. Her concern was that her daughter would feel lost, homesick and shy, while Patti knew she could cope with those feelings if only she could remain inconspicuous and be given the chance to be accepted at Ricky's for exactly what she was.

A glance at her watch told Patti that she really would have to go in now. It was a quarter past twelve and her mother would want to have the meal on the table in fifteen minutes. She still had to change, she might have to help chop up some of the herbs, and no doubt the boys would have to be summoned from a distant and unlikely playing place. She gathered up the lettuce, tomatoes, radishes and herbs that she had picked and went towards the house with the brisk but graceful and springy step that her largely outdoor upbringing had given her.

Angus Pritchard would have been very surprised by
the appearance she presented at that moment. Dressed
simply in jeans and a pink gingham shirt, with her slim
build, golden summer tan, clear blue eyes and bouncing
frenzy of blonde curls, she looked the picture of health
and youthful radiance. She had been a plump child, as
Angus remembered her, but she had long outgrown
that, and her slightly-above-average height combined
with her slimness to give her more fears about gangliness
than flab. The freckles had faded into a delicate sprink-
ling of golden dapples, and the giggles had given way to a
lively but never silly manner that was fresh and appeal-
ing.

Patti reached the house and clattered in through the
back door, silencing her movements abruptly as she
caught the sound of men's voices in the sitting-room. So
Dr Pritchard had arrived! She had missed the sound of
his car.

'Here are the vegetables, Mum.'

'Oh good!' Mrs Rainer exclaimed. 'You took your
time, dear.'

'Yes, I'm sorry. I went off into a daze,' Patti apolo-
gised briefly.

'Better run upstairs and change, then come and help
me. Angus seems to be chatting quite happily with your
father, so we can save the introductions until the boys
come in.'

Patti ducked gratefully upstairs. Dr Pritchard was
probably some pompous over-smooth medical man,
approaching middle age and beginning to thin on top,
but that didn't prevent her from wanting to make a good
impression on him. Since she had to spend this afternoon
in his company and adopt the role of his protégée, she
would look her best for it.

She reached the sanctuary of her room, peeled off her slightly damp shirt and garden-soiled jeans, dabbed some cooling eau-de-cologne over her body and put on the dress she had chosen earlier. It was frilly and feminine, and of the latest colours and length, but as she touched a brush to her hair, added filmy stockings and put on a pair of white sandals, she began to regret her choice. Something simpler and more sober would have been far better than this riotous combination of pink, peacock and white. Nothing could be done about it now, though, since all her other respectable dresses were packed.

Patti hurried downstairs again, arriving in time to dress the salad. Her three younger brothers marched noisily through the back door a minute later and were sent upstairs to render themselves a little more presentable. They were too young to have even dim memories of a previous meeting with Angus Pritchard, being evenly spaced at twelve years, ten, and eight, but Patti was now trying to conjure up a clearer picture of the man she had met about seven years ago.

He had seemed like a part of a different generation to her then, and so she was imagining him as over forty, but the masculine tones filtering faintly from the sitting-room sounded like those of a younger man.

'Leave that now, dear,' Mrs Rainer said a moment later. 'I can manage everything else. Come through and meet Angus.'

Patti followed reluctantly, having detected a fluttering tone in her mother's voice and guessing that she was a little nervous herself.

Well, I won't be! Patti determined suddenly. I don't like this situation, but I'm not going to let him see that. I'll just be cool and pleasant and try to keep out of his way as soon as this horrible afternoon is over.

Her slim shoulders were very square and firm as she entered the sitting-room, mechanically kicking into place a corner of the shaggy pile rug which was always being turned up by the door as it opened. On the far side of the room, silhouetted against a shaft of sunlight that streamed through the window a tall figure rose and stepped forward.

'Here is Patti at last, Angus,' Mrs Rainer smiled cheerfully. 'I'm sure you'll probably recognise each other a little from when we saw each other in London all those years ago.'

'Yes, of course,' Dr Pritchard murmured, coming face to face with Patti in the centre of the room.

They shook hands and produced a few polite phrases while Patti willed herself to be able to smile politely up at him without betraying a blush. She was uncomfortably conscious that her palm would be a little damp to his touch, and yet only a moment ago she had felt quite cool.

It was the sudden sight of him that had caused the change, she knew. As her eyes had been able to focus on him more clearly after he moved out of the direct light from the window, she had instantly realised that her mental image of him was going to need a great deal of adjustment.

He was much younger than she had thought he would be. In fact she discovered that her picture of him had been gradually ageing as their meeting had loomed closer until it had reached a very unlikely point. The thinning hair and incipient paunch had been pure flights of fancy from the beginning, of course.

Now, as they both took their seats awkwardly and her father handed her a ginger ale, she had to suppress a spurt of laughter. Just imagine a paunch on this man! The thing was inconceivable!

'Oh dear!' she thought. 'This is getting harder every minute. He's definitely gorgeous, and I hadn't allowed for that at all!'

It seemed even more likely that her acquaintance with him would antagonise the other student nurses now. During the desultory conversation that was taking place, she studied him covertly. He had thick chestnut hair and deep blue-green eyes, was quite finely built yet over six feet tall and obviously very capable of using his body, and had skin that was tanned so that a tendency to freckle slightly had become a very attractive outdoor textured quality.

Patti felt a shyness return which she thought she had outgrown.

'How long have you been interested in nursing, Patti?' Dr Pritchard was asking with cool politeness.

'Oh, well, um, on and off for quite a few years, really,' she replied awkwardly. 'I suppose before it was something that all girls think of—like being an air hostess—but lately I've become much more serious about it than that.'

She noticed that his well-drawn eyebrows had raised themselves slightly and wondered if the gesture had been a deliberate one. Perhaps he thought she was still in the grip of some naive, childish fantasy about nursing. His reply seemed to confirm her idea.

'I hope your enthusiasm lasts,' he said. 'Have you ever actually seen much of hospital life?'

'Well, I had to go there—to the Sir Richard—to fill in some forms, and I had my appendix out four years ago . . . And I've read a few books.'

'A fairly typical trainee, then,' he smiled. 'Like most,

I think you'll find the medical world very different from anything you've been used to.'

'Oh yes, I know that,' she jumped in, wanting to prove herself suddenly, but sounding too eager and impulsive even to her own ears. 'That's part of the attraction. Something different . . . I mean, not that it's just that . . . but the riding school—I got sick of forever doing filthy menial jobs and, well, I'll just have to see how it goes.'

She finished very lamely, feeling that her reply had lessened his opinion of her still further. I'm an adult! she thought fiercely. Why is it that I sound fourteen years old today?

A faint cynical smile still seemed to hover around the doctor's lips, as well it might after that last terrible speech, but fortunately at this moment Mrs Rainer returned to announce that the meal was served, and the awkward little group moved into the dining-room where Christopher, Timothy and Simon sat looking quite neat and well-behaved.

The boys were introduced in turn and the meal of chilled soup, cold roast beef and salad began. Dr Pritchard was still not feeling particularly relaxed. It had taken him some time to adjust his ideas about Patti Rainer to fit the picture she had presented to him as she had entered the sitting-room with a flash of youthful colour a few minutes earlier.

He had forgotten that girls could change so drastically between thirteen and twenty, and had forgotten, too, that twenty years of age was womanhood. Although obviously a little shy, Patti Rainer was definitely grown up.

But those speeches of hers about nursing had reminded him that even if her appearance bore no relation to his imagined portrait, the personality he had sketched out could well have been accurate. There had been little clarity or sense in the reasons she had given for deciding to try nursing, and he thought now with irritation that she would probably be one of those who stuck it out for only a few weeks before leaving to take a quick secretarial course.

'I found I couldn't stand the sight of blood,' he could hear her saying with a laugh. But now it was time for him to turn his attentions to his obligations as a guest.

Conversation began to progress at a steady and entertaining pace, and continued throughout the meal, although Patti said little. The boys were on their best behaviour, and Dr Pritchard seemed genuinely to enjoy drawing them into lively explanations of their messy engineering works in the stream that ran through the nearby common. The young surgeon's earlier annoyance and abstraction seemed to have dissipated now, and Patti was very thankful that the focus had shifted away from her.

After the meal she was quite content to wash the dishes with Christopher's help, while her father took Angus on a tour of their rambling garden.

'He's probably bored stiff,' Patti thought. 'But I don't care. We're obviously destined not to get on.'

It was after three when moves were made towards the surgeon's departure with his protégée. Her suitcases were loaded into the boot of his car, and he was prevailed upon to accept a final cup of tea, which occupied a further half-hour. The boys had disappeared again, but this time Mrs Rainer kept conversation going on the subject of mutual friends and acquaintances.

Patti had exchanged barely a word with the doctor since their unsatisfactory interchange before lunch, but since they had to spend a further hour or more together in the car, it was probably fortunate that they had not exhausted the limited range of subjects they would be able to discuss together.

'Well, darling,' Mrs Rainer said at last, as a signal that the moment had come.

'Yes!' Patti rose to her feet. 'I'd like to be going now, if that's all right with you, Dr Pritchard. I should give myself time to unpack properly and get an early night.'

'Of course,' the surgeon replied. 'And I have things to do at the hospital myself.'

'Do you live in, Angus?' Mrs Rainer asked.

'No, I have a flat. It's very near the hospital, but it gives me a complete break from the place, which I find I need very badly at times.'

'Yes, that's understandable for a man in your position,' Patti's mother nodded.

They had all been edging towards the door, but no one had actually left the room, so Patti decided to make the first move, picking up the handbag that lay on the hall table and walking quickly out to the car.

'The boys aren't here to say goodbye!' Mrs Rainer exclaimed.

'We said our goodbyes before, Mother,' Patti replied. 'And it's not as though I'm going far. I'll probably be home every second weekend, as we agreed.'

'I know, darling, but I can't help being a little sentimental. The first of my babies to leave the nest.'

They exchanged a warm cuddle, but Patti was faintly embarrassed in front of Dr Pritchard. He would think that an absurd fuss was being made about the whole thing. First the horrible business of being asked to introduce her to the matron, or whatever she was called, and now this exaggerated farewell. Mr Rainer squeezed

Patti's shoulders fondly for a moment, then she slid into
the front seat of the car while Angus thanked his hosts
for their hospitality and took his place at the wheel.

Silence reigned in the car for the first five minutes of
the drive. Patti wound down her window and tried to
absorb herself in the pleasant semi-rural scenery that
passed, and in the fresh scent of the air, but did not fully
succeed. By turning her head just slightly she could see
Dr Pritchard's profile quite well as he sat beside her,
apparently quite intent on the road.

He was frowning and he drove fast. Was he so very
anxious to get rid of his charge? Of course he was, and
Patti could not blame him, though perversely the very
fact that she could understand his antagonism made her
dislike the man.

'Your parents have a very nice place,' he said at last,
his well-shaped mouth forming the words without the
hint of a smile. 'You've lived there all your life, haven't
you?'

'Yes, and I love it.'

'Then you're not looking forward to living in at
Ricky's?'

'Oh, I wouldn't say that,' Patti replied seriously.
'Home is nice, but I've never been away before and I
think it is time I did. I want to find out more about
myself, and so on.'

'Yes, I suppose there is the potential for doing that at a
training hospital.'

The tone he used was dry and she felt he was making
fun of her.

'That's important!' she retorted, more angrily than
she had meant to. 'I'm twenty. I have to decide what sort
of direction my life is going to take, what I want, and
what I'm capable of, and I can't find out all those things

at home where everything is too easy. I want to challenge myself for once.'

'Sorry, I didn't mean to sound critical,' Dr Pritchard replied with a tiny hint of friendliness. But then his voice became very cool and matter of fact again. 'I don't think you should get the idea that life as a student nurse in a big hospital is anything very earth-shattering, though. You'll meet some interesting people, and some very ordinary ones, and the work you do for the first year will probably not involve the miraculous saving of life but simply the everyday care of sick people, some of whom will be very difficult to handle.'

'Of course, and that's part of what I want to find out—whether I can look after difficult people.' Patti spoke calmly, wanting to go on and ask him why he seemed to assume that she was so ignorant about what nursing involved, but biting back the words at the last minute, thinking that he would be too polite to give anything but a smooth and dishonest answer.

His reply to her last statement was commonplace and silence fell between them again for several minutes. They passed a small café much frequented by young people, and Patti noticed that the doctor slowed for a moment and looked across at it as they passed. Was he wondering if he should stop and buy coffee for her? If he was, he evidently decided not to, as in a moment he had pressed his foot on the accelerator again and showed no sign of stopping for the rest of the journey.

It was just before five when they turned in at the big formal gates of the hospital, and Angus wound carefully along the section of road which led to the nurses' home, observing the low speed limit scrupulously.

Patti felt her heart give a great lurch as she absorbed the sight of the various buildings. She had seen the place several times now, but this was the first time she had observed it so closely. She would be living here for the next three years at least. Would they be happy ones? The hospital seemed huge, a network of forbidding-looking buildings connected by covered walkways, drives, ramps and stairs. It was relatively modern in design, yet not attractive, apart from the leafy trees and plots of garden which had been placed in every possible spare space to soften the geometrical facades and give an atmosphere of peace and quiet life.

Dr Pritchard's car came to a smooth halt at the front of the nurses' home and Patti climbed out, walking automatically to the boot to help with the luggage.

'Leave that,' Angus ordered. 'We'll see Matron first, then come back for your luggage. I'm afraid I don't know what the procedure is. I've never had to check anyone into this place before, but I assume she'll have a room number and a key assigned for you.'

He sounded uncomfortable and impatient and did not wait for her as he spoke but began to stride towards the front door, assuming she would follow—which she did, of course, flushing faintly. There were half a dozen girls in the foyer. Two or three were obviously new and stood about looking as awkward as Patti felt, but there were several old hands in uniforms that were trimmed with second or third-year colours.

These girls sat in an untidy group of chairs, apparently waiting to see the secretary or Matron about something, but not in any particular hurry to get their business done. When Dr Pritchard walked briskly past they looked up, and Patti caught stares of surprise. Whispering and questioning broke out as soon as the doctor had passed, and Patti did not miss the tail-end of a speculative glance directed at herself. She guessed that the sight of the

important and good-looking young surgeon in the foyer
of the nurses' home was a rare one and that the girls
were wondering at the reason for it—and at her own
identity.

'Sister Clayton's office?' Dr Pritchard murmured
questioningly to an older woman who came out of a
corridor carrying a large bundle of keys. She was dressed
in some kind of housekeeper's uniform and pointed
without hesitation to a yellow door just beyond where
the doctor stood. Again Patti followed him, pausing a
few paces behind as he knocked and received permission
to enter.

A grey-haired woman of comfortable middle-age sat
at a neat desk and smiled as the doctor entered. They
exchanged greetings which indicated that they knew
each other slightly but not well—which was to be expected. Patti realised that their paths would not cross
often, and her awkwardness and embarrassment surged
up even more strongly than before. This whole introduction idea was ridiculous and horrible.

'Sister Clayton, this is Patricia Rainer, the daughter of
friends of mine. She is moving in here today, as you may
know, to start her training tomorrow, and I've been . . .
I thought I'd just ask you to make sure she feels at
home.' Angus Pritchard delivered the little speech
smoothly, not hinting at his reluctance, and Sister
Clayton turned to the newcomer with a welcoming
smile.

'I'm pleased to meet you, Patricia.'

'Patience,' Patti blurted out before she could stop
herself. It was a mistake that was often made with her
name, and she hated it.

'Patients? In here?' Both Sister Clayton and Dr
Pritchard looked towards the open doorway in surprise,

their medical training making them assign only one possible meaning to the awkwardly blurted word.

'No, sorry, not medical patients,' Patti explained in an agony of embarrassment. 'I mean, I'm afraid Dr Pritchard has made . . . My name is actually not Patricia, it's Patience, but it doesn't matter.'

She gave a nervous and apologetic laugh: Dr Pritchard responded with an unintelligible sound, and only Sister Clayton seemed unruffled.

'Is it really? How very pretty and unusual!' she said politely, registering no surprise at the fact that Dr Pritchard did not even seem to know the name of the girl he was supposed to be looking after. There was a small silence.

'I presume you have a room for her?' Angus Pritchard asked.

'Yes, I'll just look up my list. We've had so many new girls coming in this weekend, with the new batch of trainees starting. I don't know quite where I am this afternoon,' Sister Clayton said, turning the pages of a large ledger book that sat on her desk. 'Here we are! P. Rainer. Room 616. The sixth floor. You'll be glad we have a lift.'

'I'll stay to help with her luggage . . .' Dr Pritchard murmured, making it quite clear by his tone and by the impatient movements of his body that he had other things to do and would like to be off as quickly as possible.

Sister Clayton produced a key from the big numbered board that hung on the side wall of her office. She seemed to feel that, as a courtesy to the surgeon, she had to accompany the pair to his car, so Patti was forced to endure some even more surprised and inquisitive glances and semi-audible whispered words from the uniformed nurses as the three of them passed through the foyer twice more.

Probably Sister Clayton did not usually accompany a new girl to her room, especially on a day like today when it seemed that many others had already gone through the same procedure of arrival. And Dr Pritchard's presence would make Patti's situation even more unusual. She knew without a shadow of doubt that gossip would start about the matter, and she would be questioned on it as soon as the girls got to know her slightly.

The new room seemed neat and clean, though a little small and on the dark side of the building. Sister Clayton explained a few things and pointed to a short and very reasonable list of rules pinned to the door, then went back to her work, leaving Dr Pritchard still standing in the doorway, twitching his knee in an unconscious gesture of impatience. Patti could see that he was waiting for her to thank him as a signal for him to depart.

'I think I'll settle in here quite well now,' she said, trying to smile sincerely at him. 'Thank you for all your help, especially with the luggage and the introduction to Sister Clayton . . . I'm sure I'll get along much better here because of it.'

Again she caught the faint lift of his brows as he replied, 'Yes, I hope you do too. Don't thank me, though. It was no trouble.'

'I hope I haven't delayed you too much . . .'

'Not at all. I'll see you tomorrow morning, then.'

'Tomorrow?'

'Yes. Had you forgotten?' he queried dryly. 'You wanted to be introduced to Sister Taylor, too, the Head of Training. And, if possible, apparently, Sister Reid, the Director of Nursing as well. Though I doubt I'll have time for that one, I'm afraid.'

'Sister Taylor and Sister Reid,' Patti murmured, appalled. Her mother had talked of it, but Patti had not taken in the fact that this would involve a second specially-arranged meeting with Dr Pritchard.

And what good would it do? None at all. Sister Clayton had been friendly this afternoon, but all three of them had known, without acknowledging the fact, that the exercise had been pointless. A polite greeting, a few minutes taken out of Sister's tightly scheduled day, and all Patti would be was a very slightly more familiar face passed in the corridors of the building or glimpsed in the dining-room.

'Would it suit you if we met in the foyer tomorrow morning, ten minutes before you are due to start?' Dr Pritchard was asking. 'Then we can walk over to the training block together. What time do you start?'

'Eight-thirty, but . . .'

'I'll be in the foyer at twenty-past, then.'

'Look, if . . .'

'I have to go.' He reached out a hand to pat her briefly on the shoulder, but she moved a little and the hand slipped down her back, making the gesture like a caress, which gave her a strange uncomfortable feeling and distracted her from the final protest she was going to make—that she would really be quite happy if he didn't come tomorrow morning at all.

Angus withdrew his arm quickly, as embarrassed as Patti was.

'Good luck!' It was said coolly and quickly, then he had gone, walking briskly along the corridor to the lift.

Patti did not want to call out after him. A couple of girls had passed along the corridor and stared through the open door while she had been standing in the room with Sister Clayton and the surgeon, and she was becoming more sensitive about her acquaintance with him by the minute. Perhaps when he arrived to meet her tomorrow morning she could suggest that he needn't accompany her.

And after that, with her new busy schedule of lowly first-year duties, she would scarcely see him at all. In a few weeks he would probably pass her in a corridor without recognition, since she would be dressed in a uniform and cap identical to dozens of others.

'He'll forget my very existence,' Patti thought – and wondered why she was suddenly disappointed at the idea.

CHAPTER TWO

HE WAS already waiting for her as she hurried along to the foyer the next morning, and Patti knew he would be annoyed because she was several minutes late. Arranging her wayward hair in the rather severe style that nurses needed to wear had taken her longer than expected and the lift had been slow to arrive. She saw him before he had registered her approach, sitting awkwardly and impatiently in an uncomfortable hard-backed chair as he gazed rather moodily out of the window, evidently wishing to avoid the curious and admiring glances which his presence in the nurses' home invariably provoked.

He seemed even better looking this morning than she remembered, but there was a weariness in the lines of his face that had not been there the last time she had seen him. This would account for his impatience to leave the hospital yesterday. He had known that in a little flat somewhere a special woman was waiting for him. A man like Angus Pritchard would definitely not lack social partners. Somehow his tiredness suited him just as much as the lively smile he had—only rarely!—shown yesterday, and Patti found that again a barrier of shyness and embarrassment had already grown up in her. No doubt once again she would bungle this meeting completely . . .

'I'm so sorry I'm late,' she murmured as she stopped in front of him and caught his attention. Then she finished lamely with a few incoherent words about the lift.

Angus Pritchard stood up, startling her afresh with the tall, capable lines of his figure.

'Yes, the lifts here can be rather slow,' he agreed. 'You'll have to remember to allow for that, especially when you're on duty.'

He had begun to lead the way out of the building straight away, and Patti suddenly thought that he was probably on duty himself that morning. She blurted out the words before she could stop herself.

'I'm keeping you from your work. I feel awful. Please don't feel you have to introduce me to Sister Taylor.'

'But that's what you wanted, isn't it? Now that I'm here I might as well, and I'm not late for anything. I don't start work until eleven tonight.'

Patti digested this information in silence. He had obviously made a special trip from his flat just to go through with another farcical few minutes of politeness, and he was on the night shift tonight!

'You should have told me yesterday!' Patti exclaimed. 'If I'd known I was getting you out of bed for this . . .'

'But you didn't,' he interrupted with steely patience. 'I worked last night as well. I finished just under an hour ago and I've only had four hours' sleep since I saw you yesterday.'

'Oh.'

Then it was a heavy night's work that accounted for his tired manner, not a long evening of partying with some lovely and sophisticated woman, as Patti had supposed. Not that this meant that the lovely woman—and more than one probably—did not exist, of course. But it did bring home to Patience in yet another way how much this man's life was beyond anything she had experienced. He would have professional concerns which she had no inkling of, and with his obvious intelligence, even his free time would be spent with people who were on an altogether different plane . . .

Patti now made a few quick calculations. If he had been working on Saturday night too, before driving down to her parents' place, he might scarcely have slept since some time Saturday afternoon. Yet he had not mentioned the fact once. No wonder he had been impatient yesterday afternoon then! Every minute he had spent with her had meant a minute less sleep for him.

'I'm sorry,' she murmured ineffectually, and to her intense relief it was only a moment later that they turned into the foyer of what must be the training building.

'Dr Pritchard!' A brisk-looking woman in her late thirties detached herself from a group of student nurses and came up to them before Patti had had time to take in any impression of her surroundings. 'This is a surprise! A surgeon in the training school . . . What can we do for you? There's nothing wrong, is there?'

She seemed very pleased to see him, but was obviously a little puzzled at his presence, as Sister Clayton had been yesterday.

'No, nothing's wrong Sister Taylor,' Angus smiled charmingly. 'I'm simply here to introduce you to one of your new trainees, Patience Rainer, a friend of the family. I'm hoping you'll make her feel welcome and at home for my sake. If she has any problems, make sure I hear about them.'

He could have kicked himself! Those had not been the words he had meant to use at all. Frowning, and only dimly aware of Sister Taylor and Patti making awkward responses to each other, he reflected that it must have been weariness that had made him so careless. He really had sounded as though he wanted the girl to have special attention, when that was the last thing he had intended—and looking across at the silent bunch of trainees standing only a few yards away, he could see that they had heard every word of his speech. He thought quickly of the repercussions that the mistake might have. Resentful accusations of unprofessional favouritism, gossip that he was having an affair with the girl . . . It was also possible that other people would seek the same favour. He had bumped into his second cousin Margaret recently, and apparently her next-door neighbour's girl was planning to come here as a dietician!

The tired surgeon groaned inwardly.

'While you're here, Dr Pritchard,' Sister Taylor said brightly, interrupting his train of irritated thought, 'would you like to see our new lab for training in theatre technique? Your friend won't be using it herself for a few weeks of course, but I think it will interest you as a surgeon anyway.'

'Oh . . . er, all right,' Angus replied, not knowing how to refuse.

He didn't know Angela Taylor terribly well, but whenever he did meet her—usually in the staff dining-room or at the occasional hospital social gathering—she always displayed this over-bright eagerness to please. At the back of his mind there was the faint awareness that she probably cherished a romantic feeling about him, but such a response was not unusual. Again, not fully consciously, he had long-ago realised that the best thing to do in such cases was to ignore the fact, while at the same time being completely polite and courteous. So he added with an attempt at greater enthusiasm, 'Yes, that will be interesting.'

'Good. I'll only be able to spare a few minutes. We have a rather full programme today—we've restructured the two-month preliminary training block and it's all rather experimental. We may be trying to fit too much in and I'm not sure that Sister . . . But come this way,' Sister Taylor broke off abruptly in the middle of her chaotic explanation and led her two embarrassed visitors away from the group of nurses.

They entered a long corridor and Angus stood back for Patti to pass ahead of him, using this gallantry to distance himself from Sister Taylor's side.

'Careful of the floor. They polish it so highly. I've slipped several times,' Sister Taylor said, waving a vague hand.

Patience was stepping back in her turn at that moment, suggesting that Angus should be the one to walk at Sister Taylor's side, and her eyes met his accidentally as Sister's worry about the floor was fluttered out.

'Words of wisdom, Miss Rainer,' Angus murmured, with, unbelievably, a twinkle in his eye.

Patti suppressed a delighted laugh, returned the twinkle in full measure, then blushed and grew hot. The moment passed almost before she had had time to enjoy it and the silent conflict about who should go first was resolved by both of them setting off together behind Sister Taylor. Ridiculously, however, she could not help replaying the tiny incident over and over in her mind as they continued to follow Sister's rapid steps. Dr Pritchard had actually treated her as something other than a stupid little girl! And the sensation had been very pleasant, what's more. His eyes had been so very blue and the wry twist of his smile so very mischievous.

'Here we are!' Sister Taylor's ever-bright voice cut across Patti's unproductive thoughts.

The door was opened to reveal a fully-equipped operating theatre, complete in every detail except that it did

not contain a group of green-clad medical workers concentrated around the central table.

'We're very proud of this,' Sister Taylor said. 'There's
no reason why you couldn't come in here tomorrow,
Angus—Dr Pritchard—and perform surgery on a real
patient. Our nurses will have the opportunity to become
so familiar with the layout and routine of Theatre that
the real thing will no longer seem at all intimidating to
them when they come across it for the first time.'

'And is that really a completely positive thing?' Angus
replied. His smile took any sting of criticism out of his
words, but Patti felt that there was a serious meaning
behind his question.

'Oh, Doctor! What do you mean?'

'I mean that in a sense I will always feel . . . perhaps
not intimidated, but a little in awe of Theatre,' Angus
explained. 'I certainly never want to feel blasé or careless about it. What I am doing there is too important.'

'So you don't think this simulated theatre is a good
thing?' Sister queried with an anxious and disappointed
frown.

Patience was silent. She thought she understood that
that was not Angus's meaning—in fact, everything that
he was saying seemed entirely logical and clear to her—
but it was not her place to reply.

'Of course it's a good thing!' There was a suppressed
hint of testy impatience in his tone. 'I'm simply saying
that I hope you are not so concerned about removing
your students' irrational fears about theatre that you
remove their healthy respect for the place as well.'

'Oh, I see, yes, well of course . . . You haven't had
much of a look round yet, Patience. Feel free to take an
interest in any part of it.'

Patience was very glad to take Sister at her word and

stepped further into the room, trying not to be conscious of the fact that Angus still seemed to be watching her, although Sister Taylor had begun to chat to him about hospital affairs in the breathless way that seemed to be her signature. It would have been nicer to have been alone in this fascinating place. The occasional operating room scene on television or in films had given her no idea about the complex reality of a theatre, and she could not even guess at the function of half the apparatus and instruments she saw.

There was an atmosphere about the place too, which affected her very strongly although she could not begin to define it. Real operations had never been performed here, she gathered, but it was not hard to people the room in her mind's eye with the capable figures of surgeons and anaesthetists or the retiring ones of junior scrub nurses. She imagined Angus's lean hands delicately working over the inert form of a patient and she could hear his terse commands. 'Swab! Scalpel!' Or did people only say those things in films? She suddenly felt shockingly ignorant.

'I'm sorry, Patience, but we had better go back to the others now. We're keeping Dr Pritchard from far more important things, I'm sure . . .' Here Sister Taylor smiled up at him rather foolishly. 'And you and I can't afford to be late ourselves.'

'Of course,' Patti replied, shutting off her fascinated speculations firmly.

She felt, and was, ignorant now. But soon she would start to learn, and suddenly she felt quite hungry to do so.

Sister shepherded the two of them out of the silent theatre and shut the door, then began to lead the way back down the corridor. Patti thought she caught the tail-end of a speculative glance from Dr Pritchard directed at herself, and wondered what it could mean. Probably she had looked a fool standing there in the middle of the theatre, lost in reverie and with a finger absent-mindedly tracing the complicated angles of a movable lamp.

But if she had, it couldn't be helped. Dr Pritchard was in another world. It was becoming more and more obvious by the minute as he continued to talk in what almost seemed like a foreign language about complicated hospital affairs. In a few moments he would have left the training building—no doubt with a sigh of profound relief—and would forget her very existence.

They reached the foyer again just as the tramping of many pairs of sensible shoes signalled that the group of trainees was about to be taken to the main lecture room by Sister Moore, the deputy director of training.

'I'll have to go, and I can see that you are about to start,' Angus said abruptly. 'You'll be all right, Patience?'

'Yes, and thank you very much for . . .'

'Good,' he nodded. 'I dare say I'll be seeing you around anyway.'

'I hope so,' Patti replied with a complete lack of sincerity, and after a few more polite exchanges between the surgeon and the fluttery yet attractive Director of Training, the whole thing was over and he had gone.

Patience looked at Sister Taylor and saw a hint of disappointment register for a moment on her smooth face, but then she motioned to Patti to follow the group of girls and they both began to listen to the words of Sister Moore.

'You'll spend the first two weeks of this training period working here, both in the lecture theatre and the practical training rooms, when you will be divided into

smaller groups, and will be under the supervision
of . . .'

It was hard to concentrate at first. Patti thought back
on the previous evening and how she had spent it after
Dr Pritchard's departure. She had retired for the night at
just after ten feeling quite optimistic. The hour before
tea had been spent in unpacking and making her room as
pleasant and homey as possible, with clothes hanging in
the wardrobe or folded neatly in drawers and a few
special pictures and posters put up on the walls.

Having her meal in the large cafeteria-style dining-
room had been frightening at first, but she had chatted
briefly with two fellow trainees and had only had one
moment of mild panic when she had caught sight of a
tall, chestnut-haired figure which she had thought for a
moment was Dr Pritchard—and then it had turned out
not to be him after all. Her mood as she drifted into sleep
had actually been one of excitement and anticipation
and she had just experienced the feeling again as she had
stood in the training theatre. But none of it remained
now.

Although most of the girls had been listening to Sister
Moore, some had glanced with obvious curiosity at Patti
as she had joined the group, and she knew that the fact
that she had received special attention both from Sister
Taylor and the handsome surgeon would not have gone
unnoticed. Nothing could be achieved by worrying
about it now, though.

After two hours of very practical introductory explanation by Sister Taylor, beginning at eight forty-five
when the group of sixty were all seated in the lecture
hall, there was a short break for morning coffee—and it
was then that the first questions about Dr Pritchard
began. One of the girls Patience had talked to the

previous evening came up to her.

'I envy you with that gorgeous doctor for a boyfriend!' she exclaimed.

'He's not my boyfriend, Alison,' Patti replied, a quick flush staining her cheek.

'Really?' The dark and rather sharp-faced girl gave her a disbelieving sidelong glance. 'Come on, you don't have to pretend! He virtually admitted it. "Make her feel welcome for my sake, make sure I hear about any problems she has."'

'Yes, I know, I don't know why he said that.' Patti was trying to keep her voice as low as possible but the other girl was speaking very audibly and the heads of several trainees had turned as they sipped their coffee.

'Well, if I were you, there's only one way I'd take it,' Alison giggled. 'He must fancy you. Just wait, you'll get paged at the nurses' home and he'll be on the phone for you, asking you out.'

'Don't be silly!' Patti was goaded to reply. There had been a couple of girls associated with the riding school whose only topic of conversation had been men, but Patti had always resisted being drawn into their circle. Oh, it was not that she was cold or a loner. In fact, she had had one or two casual boyfriends in the past and cherished some very warm and secret dreams about the future, but it was for this very reason that she did not want to enter into Alison's discussion now. If a special person did enter her life, his name was not going to be bandied about by a dozen girls.

'I'm not being silly,' Alison replied indignantly. 'I thought you'd be pleased to think a man like Dr Pritchard would be interested in you. You're pretty enough, apart from looking so young, but perhaps that appeals to him.'

'Listen, he's just a friend of the family. I barely know him, so please don't let's talk about it any more,' Patti said desperately.

But Alison was not to be side-tracked so easily.

'A friend of the family! I wish my family had friends like that!'

'Oh I don't think Dr Pritchard is all that gorgeous,' another girl put in, tossing a set of red curls.

'Don't you?' Alison turned to her. 'I do! And he'd have a lot of money to spend on a girl as well, with a surgeon's pay.'

'There are other good-looking surgeons at the hospital,' the redhead replied. 'My sister has been nursing here for two years now, and she's got a horrific crush on Dr Bentley in the renal unit. She pointed him out to me yesterday and my God, I can see what she means!'

Patti tried to take this opportunity to extract herself from the discussion by pretending to be in search of a biscuit to eat with her coffee, but Alison spoke to her again before she could.

'If you don't want him for yourself, I'd be more than happy to take him off your hands, my dear,' she drawled. 'Feel free to arrange an introduction any time.'

'Please, let's not talk about it like that,' Patti begged. She could see Sister Moore chatting with a group of girls on the far side of the room and was certain that she would try and say a word to all the trainees during this break. If she came across now and caught this conversation, Patti would want to sink through the floor. Being man-mad was exactly the reputation she did *not* want to acquire here at Ricky's, at the start of what she hoped would be a serious and long-term career.

'I don't think I'll be seeing him, but if I do I'll introduce you, all right?' she promised rashly, willing to try anything to close the subject. But of course, the promise only excited Alison further.

'Will you really? I'll probably faint! It would be my dream come true if I could go home to Bristol and tell my friends I was going out with a surgeon.'

Patti wanted to retort that she herself had slightly more noble ambitions for her future at Ricky's, but she did not want to make an enemy of Alison, so she wisely said nothing. Shortly after this Sister Moore did come over and the embarrassing subject of Angus Pritchard was at last closed, but Patti realised with a sigh that it would be brought up again and again unless she could find a way of squashing people's interest once and for all.

The rest of the day's programme distracted Patti from these worries quite successfully, however. It seemed so long since she had done any serious study, and she found that she was already enjoying the task of putting her brain into activity. Of course, the first day was devoted to comparatively light matters, but still Patti felt that she had been given an appetising taste of what was to come.

At lunch-time most girls seemed to be too involved in discussing what had happened that morning to question Patti more closely about her relationship with Dr Pritchard, although she did notice one or two cast a slightly speculative or apprehensive glance in her direction, and once someone asked her a very involved question about how much paperwork surgeons had to do and who they were responsible to in the hospital administration. Of course, she had absolutely no idea of these matters and the question worried her. Were these girls simply taking it for granted that she was heavily involved with Angus Pritchard? It was the kind of story which could be spread so easily throughout the hospital and which her denials would have no power to stop. Feeling suddenly older and wiser, Patti reflected that of course people found it much more interesting to believe a piece of gossip and pass it on than to spread the word that there was nothing in it after all.

Alison sat with her at tea that evening and obviously still had the attractive surgeon on her mind.

'Did you mean what you said at morning break about introducing me to Dr Pritchard?' she asked in a confiding whisper. They were seated with two or three other trainees at a long, noisy table mostly made up of ancillary staff.

'Oh . . . er, yes I suppose so,' Patti mumbled, her heart sinking.

'Because he's sitting just over there,' Alison said.

Patti's head flew round in the direction of Alison's pointing finger and she blushed hotly, but could see no sign of the surgeon.

'Caught you!' Alison crowed. 'You do fancy him, I thought so. No, he isn't sitting there, but if he does come in, please let me at least meet him!'

'Yes, I will, but please can we close the subject?' Patti said, disliking the girl more every minute. With her dark curly hair, large green eyes, and vivacious manner, Alison was someone who probably found it relatively easy to attract men. If she wanted to, she would be able to be a very lively companion, and in the company of someone she liked, the hint of sharpness in her features would be toned down.

I wonder if a man like Dr Pritchard would be attracted to her, Patti thought—and pulled her thoughts up abruptly as she realised what lay behind the question. He wouldn't like Alison, her heart had responded instantly. He's too upright and discerning for that. Yet she had no basis for thinking that about him, when they had only met so briefly and awkwardly. *Did* she fancy him, as Alison had teasingly suggested? No, of course she didn't! She was willing to acknowledge that he was very good-looking, but anyone would have to admit that. But what she felt about him as a person was dislike, pure and simple, after the embarrassment he had caused her—and it was an opinion that she would not change!

Patti brought her attention back to the concrete present as she realised that Lisa, one of the other girls in the group, was speaking to her.

'What did you think of the lectures today?'

'Oh, I found them interesting, didn't you?' Patti responded, very eager to talk about the day, both to get away from the nagging question of Dr Pritchard and because she had been genuinely stimulated by the things they had been told.

'Yes, I did,' Lisa replied. 'Especially in the afternoon. What about you, Alison?'

'Oh, I was a bit bored, to tell you the honest truth,' the dark-haired girl replied. 'Most of it was just common sense, and the rest of it you can just crib up on from textbooks.'

'Did you think so?' Lisa queried with a frown. 'I thought it was all linked together in a way that made it very new to me.'

'Yes, I suppose so. I wasn't listening very closely. I'll probably concentrate on it more tomorrow. I always find it very difficult to settle down to something on the first day,' Alison explained vaguely, her gaze fixed on a nearby table where several young orderlies were laughing loudly.

Patti caught Lisa's eye and found that her own distrust of Alison's attitude was reflected there. I don't like

Alison much, but I think Lisa will turn out to be nice, she decided.

This impression was confirmed as the days of preliminary training passed and the tentative overtures they had made towards each other firmed into a very rewarding friendship. By avoiding any of the girls, including Alison, who seemed too interested in the purely social aspects of their new lives as nurses, Patience managed to ignore any repercussions from the awkward first day of her training. She heard Dr Pritchard's name often—more often it seemed, than the names of most of the other doctors—but she saw him only occasionally in the distance.

He did not eat in the hospital dining-room with predictable regularity as many of the surgeons did. Patti told herself she was relieved, but sometimes she did think it would be nice to see that wry, twinkling smile again—until she reflected that Angus was not likely to bestow many such smiles on her, even if they did meet. After ten days of preliminary training, she was beginning to congratulate herself that her inauspicious beginning were not going to affect life and work here at Ricky's after all . . .

CHAPTER THREE

'PATIENCE RAINER to the phone, please. Would Nurse Rainer please come to the phone if she is in?'

The paging announcement cut across the sound of the television in the recreation lounge where Patti was relaxing one evening with a small group of nurses who had formed themselves into an 'informal self-help knitting clib' as Lisa described it.

'Leave it here, I'll look after it,' another girl, Janice, said as Patti hurriedly laid down the rather complicated lacy-patterned garment she was struggling with.

'Thanks,' Patti replied. 'It'll be my parents. Mother said she'd ring this week to arrange how I'm to get home for the weekend.'

She started towards the door but tripped over her wool, having failed to notice that it was twisted round her leg. Disentangling herself took, as it usually does, longer for the very reason that she was anxious to do it quickly, and she ended up dashing rather dangerously along the corridor to the phone booth near the lift, afraid that Reception would conclude she wasn't in and would tell her mother to ring later.

'Patience Rainer speaking.'

'Nurse Rainer? Good, I'll put you through,' the receptionist said briskly, making the connection with a click.

'Mother? Sorry, I was knitting and got tangled in my wool,' she gasped breathlessly. 'You were right about the pattern, it's terribly difficult, but Janice is a real expert so she's helping me.'

'Is this Patience Rainer?' An undeniably cold and very masculine voice greeted this garbled explanation and Patti's heart sank into her shoes. It certainly wasn't her father. It was a much younger voice, and it was deeper too.

'Oh, I'm terribly sorry!' she exclaimed in an agony of embarrassment.

'This is Angus Pritchard.'

'Yes, I know. I thought it was my mother,' Patti explained unnecessarily.

'So I gather. Perhaps you had better ring her later yourself if you are disappointed.'

'Oh, I'm not disappointed. I mean . . . it's not that . . . well, it doesn't matter,' she said very lamely.

'Would you come out for coffee with me? Are you free tonight?' he said rather bluntly, ignoring her attempts at an apology, and destroying with his words any self-control she had managed to gain.

'Coffee? That would be . . . very nice.' She checked herself just in time from expressing an enthusiasm which he would have found strange—and which, when she thought about it, she found strange herself.

He was only asking her out of duty, and she could not imagine that they would find much to say to each other when he thought her a frivolous little girl and she thought him cold and arrogant. In fact she began to wonder why she had accepted the invitation. Before he could reply, she changed her tone completely and added to her previous response.

'Except I don't think I can. I have some things to do tonight, and I don't want to be out too late . . .'

'I won't keep you too late.' He sounded quite grim. 'And I think you can give up an evening in front of the television for once, can't you?'

'How did you know that I was . . . ? Oh yes, of course, when I thought you were my mother,' she murmured incoherently.

'I'll pick you up outside the front entrance of your building in five minutes,' he cut across her words and, saying a brief goodbye, had hung up before she could catch her breath enough to point out that she hadn't actually agreed to his invitation yet.

It was certainly the coolest way such a proposal had ever been put to her. The boys she had been out with before had always been very polite and deprecating, and if Angus supposed that she found his masterful abruptness attractive and exciting, then he was very much mistaken!

But then, of course, she remembered, he wasn't setting out to be attractive. This whole thing was only what he saw as his duty from start to finish. She should have told him straight away that he needn't have bothered.

Patience had not been standing idly in the phone booth as she thought all this. He had, after all, given her only five minutes to dress. Having felt tired after the day's lectures and practical work had finished at five, she had peeled off a slightly crumpled uniform and stepped with relief into casual corduroy pants of a dusky pink, topped with a comfortable cotton shirt and dark brown pullover. For a quiet evening in the nurses' residence the combination had been neat, pretty and perfectly adequate, but for coffee at an unknown café or wine bar in the company of an elegant surgeon, it was definitely not.

Patti surveyed herself in the mirror and decided that the cord jeans would have to stay, but she would put on her short black boots, a full-sleeved blouse of cream satin and a softly-styled jacket of burgundy panne-velvet. She was already dashing back down the corridor as she flicked a comb distractedly through her hair . . .

Even so, he was already there when she arrived in the foyer. He had not bothered to come in, which Patti thought rude, but was sitting in his Rover directly outside the entrance, tapping his fingers impatiently against the rim of the steering wheel.

'I hope I'm not late,' she said with an edge as she pulled open the front door and slid in beside him.

'Not very,' he replied.

'You didn't give me very much time.'

'I suppose not.'

'Or very much choice about whether I came at all.'

Her words would have had a cutting dignity if her voice hadn't risen above its usual surprisingly mature pitch. He did not deign to reply, however, and they drove in silence out of the grounds and made several turns along quiet back streets before emerging on to a slightly busier street where coloured lights advertised a pleasant-looking coffee house that Patti and her new nursing friends had not yet discovered during their leisure-time explorations of the district.

It was a week-night, and Dr Pritchard found a parking place very nearby, reversing into it with speedy expertise. Patti risked a sidelong glance at his face as he turned, laid a long arm along the back of the seat and used his other hand to manipulate the wheel. He was still frowning. The man certainly believed in rationing those smiles of his! Perhaps he thought they acquired more value that way. Or more power.

'You didn't have to do this,' Patti ventured. 'I've already told my parents that you've made everything wonderfully easy for me at the hospital.'

Her words contained a bite of sarcasm, as she thought of how in fact he had done the opposite, even if the trouble he had caused her seemed to be dying down a bit now.

'You've told your parents? You seem to be enjoying telling a lot of people.' He climbed quickly out of the car as he spoke and Patti followed suit, wishing she could think of some clever retort to that last remark, whatever it had meant. The evening was turning out to be even more unpleasant than she had expected. What was the point of asking her for coffee if he wasn't even going to pretend that he enjoyed it?

'We'll sit here, shall we?' Angus led the way to the darkest and quietest corner of the coffee house, giving Patience no chance to say that she would have preferred a brighter table by the window. 'There may be people here from the hospital, and I don't think either of us would want to have our conversation overheard.'

In a different tone, the words could have been those of a lover suggesting a romantic tête-à-tête, but Angus Pritchard definitely did not mean them that way. In fact, his manner was so grim that Patti had a sudden feeling of fear.

'What will you have?' he asked tersely, taking her by surprise. She hadn't even begun to think about ordering, but he was obviously waiting for a prompt reply.

'Oh . . . white,' she stammered.

He did not wait for someone to come and take their order, but walked purposefully to the bar and asked for the two coffees—a black and a white. They were brought almost immediately—perhaps the staff had been intimidated by his steely gaze just as Patti was—and so a moment later they were both seated, alone together at the small table.

'I heard something yesterday which made me very angry,' Angus said without preamble, after taking a purposeful sip of the strong aromatic brew.

'Did you?' Patti replied uncertainly. She regretted her own choice of coffee. Although it was rich and good, she could not enjoy its bitterness in this mood. Something more soothing like tea or chocolate would have been much better.

'Don't pretend that you don't know what I mean. I brought you here so we could discuss the matter without causing embarrassment to you, but I'm not going to tolerate your prevarication.'

This time Patti was silent, even though his pause was manifestly designed to be filled by her own words. Something of her genuine confusion seemed to penetrate him because he did not press her, but continued himself in a more gentle tone.

'I'd like you to explain this, Patience. Yesterday I was called into the office of a very senior member of the hospital staff and was told that if I had to be romantically involved with a first-year student nurse, I ought to at least stop her from boasting about the fact, and about the special treatment she was getting in her course because of it. And there was more than a hint that an official reprimand might follow if the rumours were investigated and found to be true. I was as flabbergasted as you appear to be . . .' The word 'appear' was given an ironic emphasis. 'I asked Dr Bromfield for more details and he said that all the student nurses and many other junior members of staff were said to be talking about Patience Rainer in first-year block, and how her boyfriend—myself—had more or less ordered Training Sister to pay you special attention and mark your work favourably.'

'Isn't that your own fault?' Patti retorted now, seizing on the last part of his angry speech. 'You were the one who told Sister Taylor to contact you if I had any problems.'

'That was a polite piece of nothing, Patience, as you must realise as well as Sister Taylor would have done. This ridiculous story has grown up around something more than those words of mine. Dr Bromfield asked me if you and I were engaged. Apparently you've told some people that we are.'

'That is the most ridiculous, unjust and embarrassing thing I have ever heard!' Patti burst out, goaded beyond endurance.

'I agree, but is it true?' Angus put in smoothly. 'Have you been saying such things? I can only assume that you have, because rumours don't start from nothing.'

'Of course I wouldn't humiliate myself by saying anything of the kind!' Patti exclaimed, suddenly in full control in spite of her fury.

Although she did not know it, the angry pink of her cheeks and the flash of her blue eyes made her look positively beautiful and the slim length of her body, which she so often thought made her clumsy and gangling, was transformed into a delicately regal bearing. Angus was impressed in spite of himself and some of the hardened dislike which had fortified his cold anger dissipated. He maintained a cool façade, however.

'So you are really saying that you are not responsible for all this?'

'Certainly not! I only wish I'd heard the stories myself. I would soon have told the truth.'

'Then perhaps we can work out together what has been going on.'

'I hope so,' Patti said with spirit. 'Because if such

stories are going round as you say, then they are as embarrassing for me as they are for you, if not more so.'

'You think so? Perhaps you have a point.' Angus leaned back thoughtfully.

There was a small pause. The flare-up between them had happened so quickly, and Angus's cold manner on the telephone and in the car had not fully prepared Patti for the long accusation that had followed, so it was only now, when the surgeon's anger against her seemed to have died down, that she could catch her breath a little.

'I think I can guess what has happened,' she said now, slowly.

'Then please tell me.' A faint edge still persisted in Angus's tone, as though he wasn't yet quite prepared to believe that they both felt the same. Patti sighed and launched into her explanation.

'It's one particular girl. I won't say her name. She's quite man-mad, and when she overheard what you said to Sister Taylor she assumed I was going out with you and simply wouldn't believe me when I tried to deny it. She would love the thrill of a secret romance with a surgeon herself, and it hasn't occurred to her that that might be the last thing *I* would want!'

The delicate moue of distaste and the frown that rested for a moment on Patti's forehead did not escape Dr Pritchard's notice. 'She has a group of friends who seem to think of nothing but which staff member is involved with which, and I can't bear that sort of thing. I soon found other friends and thought that by steering clear of that group of girls and never so much as mentioning your name the talk would all die down, but apparently it hasn't. And since I've stayed away from the gossip scene and kept busy with study, I haven't heard what people are saying.'

Angus did not speak at once. Patti wondered if he would believe her. In a way it didn't matter a bit if he did not.

I don't care what his personal opinion of me is, she thought to herself, perhaps too fiercely, as long as it doesn't affect my training, and my friendships.

'It's a convincing explanation and I believe it,' Angus said at last, making Patti's heart lurch with relief in spite of her recent thought. 'I'll tell your story to the people who matter and then, like you, I'll just have to trust that it will all die down eventually.'

'Surely it will have to?' Patti murmured.

'It will—if we are careful not to fuel the story with any more evidence,' Angus replied lightly but firmly. 'So I suggest that we don't linger over this coffee—much as I might otherwise enjoy your company.'

He worded the token compliment in an exaggeratedly flowery way that infuriated Patti once again. He hadn't needed to say that! But there would be no point in making a retort, even if she could think of one—which for the moment she couldn't.

Angus watched while she drained without enjoyment the last mouthfuls of her coffee and then got immediately to his feet. Patti might have found his haste almost comical if she hadn't felt so strongly that his point about not adding more evidence was simply an excuse. Basically, he just didn't like her.

'And the feeling is mutual!' she said under her breath as they walked to the car.

'I beg your pardon?' He had caught the murmured words.

'Nothing.'

'There's one thing which would scotch the rumours once and for all,' he said after a moment, when they were seated in the car.

'What is that?'

'If we were both seen out with other people.' Suddenly there was that rare and surprising crooked grin.

'Yes, I suppose so,' she smiled back, not really taking the remark too seriously.

'There are plenty of unattached men at the hospital. You should find it quite easy to attract someone's interest.'

'Don't bother with compliments, please,' Patti replied shortly, hating him again. That cool over-confident tone!

'I don't mean it as a compliment. I was simply stating a fact. And since we both agree that it's a good idea, why don't you try and find someone?'

'You are unspeakable! Why don't you follow your own advice? Be seen out with someone else yourself!'

'I fully intend to.'

To that statement there was simply no reply, so they sat in silence until Angus turned expertly into the hospital driveway and slowed in front of the nurses' home.

'I'm going away in a week's time, by the way,' he said, just as Patti was about to murmur a conventional and insincere thank-you before escaping from his company.

'Oh?'

'Yes, for three weeks' holiday in Spain. That's another thing which should cool off these wretched rumours, thank goodness.'

'All right. Well, I'll see you when you get back then,' Patti replied unthinkingly, occupied internally with wondering why the knowledge that there was no chance of running into him seemed suddenly to have taken a little of the spice out of life at the hospital. His reply reminded her that she was being ridiculous.

'Don't count on it.' The tone was light and flippant but she could see that he meant it. He was seriously going to avoid her. 'I'm sorry about the evening,' he added more gently. 'Not a pleasant outing, and you won't even be able to tell anyone about it because of what we've agreed.'

'That doesn't matter.'

'But perhaps you've learnt now,' his tone had changed once more, 'that trying to get ahead or gain advantages by knowing the right person doesn't really work.'

At this Patti was so consumed with indignation that she was rendered completely speechless, and when she picked up her bag and got out of the car it was all she could do to wish him a strangled good night. It was ridiculous! One minute the man was being reasonably pleasant, to the point where she had actually felt disappointed to find that he was going away, and the next minute he squashed her again as if she was fourteen years old!

Back on the sixth floor she could hear the 'knitting club' girls still chatting away in front of the television in the recreation lounge. If she went to her room and changed back into the casual blouse and pullover—why had she bothered to change out of them in the first place!—she could be back with them less than an hour after she had left. Very likely a brief manufactured explanation about a phone call from her mother would quiet any questions about her absence.

Perhaps she could say that she had had to write quickly to an aunt who was ill, or some such tale, and then, as Dr Pritchard had so evidently desired, no one need know that they had been in each other's company that evening at all.

Dr Pritchard . . . Without really intending or wanting to, Patti began to wonder how he would pass the rest of this unsatisfactory evening. He was probably already setting in motion his little plan for being 'seen around' with somebody else. The arrogance of the man! Yet no doubt his confidence was not misplaced. There probably *were* three or four women who would jump as soon as he lifted a finger.

But as it happened, Patience was wrong about Angus's activities during the rest of the evening. After dropping her off at the hospital he had driven directly and rather wearily to his nearby flat and had pottered around his tiled kitchen preparing himself a light, late supper. Surprisingly he didn't feel terribly hungry, but he knew he ought to eat.

Somehow he felt uncomfortable about the exchange with Patience—uncomfortable about the whole outing, when he thought about it. It had been wrong of him to assume immediately that the whole thing was her fault, even though the facts had seemed against her.

Angus found that he was reviewing each of the three occasions they had met and he realised that they all had something in common. Each time he had been forced to modify his dislike of her. Firstly her manner had been so much more attractive than he had predicted, with none of the giggles and gush he would have expected. And the next day, when Sister Taylor had shown them the training theatre, Patience's fascination with the place had been evident and genuine. And lastly, tonight, there had been a dignity and honesty in her explanation which belied the personality he was still semi-consciously holding in his mind . . .

Damn it all, he thought finally. He didn't want to like the girl, did he?

For Patti, the two months of preliminary training passed very quickly and for the most part enjoyably. During this time the trainees were taught many of the basic aspects of nursing care, including hygiene, admission and charting procedures and bed-making, a skill which Patti felt at times she would never master.

Although not an untidy child, at home she had always had trouble with making her bed and had become used to sleeping in a tangle of sheets and blankets which would become progressively untidier as the night wore on.

'But I suppose after a while I'll be able to do hospital corners with my eyes closed,' she sighed to dark-haired Lisa as they walked back to the training building after lunch on their final day of preliminary block.

'I'm going to be careful not to boast too much about my new skills when I go home,' Lisa replied lightheartedly, serene in her possession of the unofficial award for Champion Bed-maker of the course. 'I've told you about my six younger brothers and sisters, haven't I? You can imagine how much my mother would enjoy giving me a busman's holiday, getting me to do all six beds for them!'

'Tell her you failed that part of the course,' Patti suggested.

'Are you kidding? Then she'd say I needed the practice and I'd have to do hers and Dad's as well!'

'My biggest fear is that I'll drop a full bedpan at the feet of some distinguished surgeon,' Patti said.

'Quite normal, my dear girl. I've had three nightmares about it already,' Lisa replied.

On this cheerful note the girls arrived in the foyer and went straight to the lecture hall which, though so strange and forbidding on the first day when all its features and the other students who filled it were new, had now become as familiar as the classrooms of schooldays. Patti did feel a slight thrill of anticipation today though, as she took her place in one of the third row seats next to Lisa and Janice. In ten minutes she would know, as they all would, which ward she would work on for the next three months.

The room filled quickly and a few minutes later Sister Taylor stood on the slightly raised platform at the front with the all-important list in her hands. Patti had warmed to the Director of Training quite a bit since that first unfortunate day. When lecturing or taking practical sessions, she was cheerful, lucid and helpful, and it seemed to be only an awkward form of shyness which sometimes showed itself in the over-bright and flustered manner Patience had reacted against at first.

Now Sister Taylor looked up from her list, checked that everyone had taken a seat and smiled, as if she could remember with perfect clarity how important the assignment of her first ward had seemed to her.

'The list is in alphabetical order, everyone,' she said. 'Your name comes first, followed by the ward name and description, then a group number which will tell you where you will be for the rest of the afternoon. We are dividing you up according to what type of ward you have been assigned, so you will then be able to ask questions and we hope we will solve any problems you have. Now, listen carefully.'

Sister Taylor paused briefly, waiting for a few isolated whispers to die away, then began to read the list of fifty-eight names.

'Adams, Jane, Digby Ward—Male Orthopaedics, Group A. Addison, Thomas, Gardner Ward—Cardiac Unit, Group C.'

Patti sat back. Her name would come towards the end of the list. But she listened for the names of her friends, caught their eyes and saw that both looked reasonably pleased with what had come their way— a female medical ward for Lisa, and Paediatrics for Janice.

'Rainer, Patience, Jackson Ward—Male Surgical, Group B.'

Well, that was all right too. She would start to learn about pre- and post-operative care, and then when she had her turn in Theatre later on, the experience would stand her in good stead.

It was afterwards when everyone was filing out to join their sub-groups in a smaller room that Patti felt a tap on her shoulder and turned to see Alison Reed pushing forward to reach her. Patti was a little surprised, as the two were really only on nodding terms now, since Patti's dislike of the girl had been fortified by the evening with Dr Pritchard when she discovered the gossip that Alison had been spreading.

Then the reason for Alison's interest became evident.

'So you *did* get a surgical ward! Did you have to ask for it specially, or was it just coincidence?'

'I don't know what you mean,' Patti replied— although she could begin to guess. Her heart sank.

'Don't you indeed!' Alison crowed. 'I'm talking about your friend Angus, of course. He'll be in and out of that ward the whole time.'

'How many times do I have to tell you that he has nothing to do with me at all!' Patti exclaimed. 'I haven't even seen him for weeks.'

'I know. He's been in Spain. Didn't you get a post-card?'

Patti was about to make another angry retort when she saw a wicked glint in the other girl's eye and realised that Alison was enjoying the way her teasing was arousing Patti's anger. So instead she said nothing at all and turned away, just as Alison herself caught sight of another friend and called out to her.

'I'm on Stafford Ward, Barbara! Don't you envy me? I'll be taking orders from that delicious Gordon Llewellyn.'

But Alison's words had left their mark. Of course she was right. Dr Pritchard would be making frequent visits to Jackson Ward. Patti knew that she was too aware of the fact that he had returned from his holiday nearly three weeks ago now. Was it with trepidation or hope that she was semi-consciously on the look-out for him every time she walked through the hospital grounds or into the staff dining-room?

And why had she grown hot the few times she had caught sight of him? Whether it was her unwilling acknowledgement of his devastating good looks or her dislike of his manner that was uppermost in her mind, she was very much afraid that she would not be able to work with clear-headed efficiency when he was on the ward.

Should she perhaps request a change? Sister Taylor had announced that it was possible to do so if you had a valid reason, and Patti saw two girls and a rather shy young man approach the Sister now. But what could her own valid reason be? She hadn't one. That was obvious immediately. In any case, Patti thought, to do such a thing would be distinctly cowardly.

When you fall off a horse, you must get straight back

on, she said to herself. Perhaps the rule was not particularly applicable in this case, but thinking it made her feel braver anyway. No, of course she wouldn't ask to change!

And she would face the disturbing Dr Pritchard and the embarrassing memories he provoked with as much dignity and coolness as she could muster!

CHAPTER FOUR

ALONG WITH most of the other trainees, Patti had been put on a morning shift for her first week of ward duty. During this first year of training, every Wednesday would be spent away from the ward, back in the training building where nurses would increase their theoretical knowledge, practise complicated procedures which they would later try on the ward, and generally reinforce and complement everything they picked up through practical experience.

The morning shift at Ricky's began at seven and Patti arrived at the main building several minutes too soon, having risen absurdly early in her anxiety to be punctual. She was glad now about the rule which required trainee nurses to wear their uniform, including cap, during the preliminary training period. It had seemed a little un-necessary at first, but with so many unfamiliar things about to happen today, she was glad that at least she felt at home in the simply-cut white dress. The action of twisting her fluffy blonde hair into a plain knot high on her head was now second nature to her too, when at first it had seemed to be tumbling down every minute.

The morning began confusedly but not unpleasantly. Later, in her memory, some things would stand out clearly and others would be just a fog.

Hazel Gibson, the senior sister in charge of three other wards as well as Jackson, met Patience and two of her fellow trainees in the foyer of the main building. She conducted each of them to their wards and introduced them to the ward sister before returning to her usual supervisory duties.

Rosemary Watson was the Sister in charge of this shift on Jackson Ward. Patti noted the quiet friendliness of her smile and the neat way that dozens of fine plaits hugged her well-shaped dark head under the immaculate white arc of her cap, and decided that there was a good chance they would get on well.

'We're glad to have you on the ward, Nurse Rainer— or shall we use first names straight away?' were Sister Watson's first words after Sister Gibson had left.

'First names, please,' Patti responded at once. 'I'm going to have to steel myself not to jump and drop things when doctors shout "Nurse!" at me. I'd rather not have to do the same with you.'

'I know the feeling,' Rosemary laughed in reply. 'Now come through here and we'll talk for a while.'

She led the way into the private atmosphere of the nurses' station, leaving the two auxiliaries, Carole and Sandra, who had also been briefly introduced to Patti, to continue with their morning routine.

The next fifteen minutes were spent in explanation of the general routine of the thirty-bed ward, and a tour of the facilities occupied a further half-hour. Then it was down to work in real earnest, as Patti was slotted straight into ward routine with a round of temperature, blood pressure and pulse measurements.

'Doctors' morning rounds usually start at half-past nine,' Rosemary had said quite casually in the middle of her description of a typical day's events on Male Surgical. Patti had nodded equally casually in reply, but she was conscious now that images of Dr Pritchard were hovering at the edge of her thoughts, and she was glad that concentrating on numbers and measurements would force such ridiculous things aside completely.

'You'll be all right with your obs, won't you?' Rosemary asked. 'Observations, I should say. It's dreadful the way we abbreviate everything.'

'It's all right. I understood what you meant,' Patience laughed.

'You see, I have other things I ought to be doing.'

'Of course I'll be all right,' Patti replied. 'Perhaps I won't be terribly quick at first, but we've learnt all about it.'

'Good. Start here and then come across to the other side where I'll be, and we'll do the annexe section of the ward together last of all.' Sister Watson smiled another one of her very reassuring smiles and walked away to the other side of the ward with a soft firm tread, which Patti knew she would have to practise!

The trolley of equipment was waiting in its place so Patti took a deep breath and wheeled it carefully to the bedside of her first patient . . .

Half an hour later the faint thrill of nervousness had already died down and she was progressing steadily down the ward. So far each of the patients had responded well to her greeting and had not seemed disturbed or irritated by her activities. She realised, of course, that for many of them the procedure was a far more familiar routine than it was for her!

She lost track of time altogether, although she was looking at her watch every minute as she timed pulses and waited the obligatory two minutes while the mercury rose in thermometer tubes. It was simply that only the second hand was necessary.

'Good morning, Mr Simkins. I'm Nurse Rainer, Patti Rainer, and I've just come to take your temperature, pulse and blood pressure.'

'Oh, no, I don't think so, love,' the old man replied, knocking her tentative confidence off balance suddenly with this completely unexpected reply, especially since it was accompanied by a rather benevolent and almost pitying smile.

'I beg your pardon?'

'I'm not to have me temperature taken, or the other things. Doctor's special orders. So you can be getting along to the next bed.'

'Oh, I see.'

Patti looked along to the next bed, as if something there would be able to confirm old Mr Simkins' confident assertion, but its occupant lay with his eyes closed. James Warner, the young man she had just been with, was due to go to theatre for a biopsy that morning and was trying to distract his nervous thoughts with reading, so he had not heard Mr Simkins' protest either.

'Really, Sister! Doesn't it say so on me chart, or me card? "No temp, pulse or b.p.", something like that.' He had called her Sister, but she was by now too flustered to correct him.

'I don't think so. I'll check again.'

Patience fumbled with the chart book and sheaf of cards she had picked up. Mr Simkins' ought to be on top but it wasn't . . . She put the chart book back on the trolley and somehow at that moment the cards slid from her hands and fanned out chaotically on the polished vinyl-tiled floor.

It was just as she was bending down to try to gather them up, already flushed, that a male voice spoke rather coldly at her side.

'What seems to be the trouble, Nurse?'

Angus Pritchard, of course, Patience thought bitterly. Why couldn't it have been some benevolent, fatherly surgeon who would have understood that first-year nurses can't always remain cool, instead of this supercilious young . . . coxcomb!

'I dropped the cards, Dr Pritchard. I'm sorry.' She was unsure whether to continue bending to pick them up, or straighten to greet him properly and leave the unfortunate things where they were.

He solved the problem for her by sliding the cards into a neat pile with the polished leather toe of an Italian shoe.

'Fortunately both our floors and my shoes are clean,' he said, and before Patti could gather the cards up, he had bent down himself, collected them without a wasted movement and handed them back to her.

For a moment she caught the faint essence of his aftershave, a musky flavour that was mingled with a hint of male warmth. He was standing far too close for comfort. She dared to glance at him and then wished she had not. That face, newly tanned from his three weeks in Spain, had not softened.

'But actually it wasn't the cards I meant,' he said. 'I wondered if you . . . were confused about Mr Simkins' treatment.'

Patti noted how he carefully worded the question to exclude any hint of criticism of the patient himself. This was as it should be, of course, but she could not help feeling that Dr Pritchard positively enjoyed suggesting that she was at fault.

'I wasn't sure whether I should take his temperature and pulse,' Patti improvised. 'You see, he . . .'

'But of course you should,' Dr Pritchard replied before she had finished. 'It's routine, and I can see no reason to depart from normal practice in this case.'

'Just what I said meself,' the old man put in complacently.

Patience shot him a glowering glance, which—probably fortunately—neither he nor the doctor saw. Rosemary Watson came up to them at that moment.

'Sorry, Doctor, I didn't realise you had arrived,' she said.

'That's all right, Sister Watson. Nurse Rainer and I have just been clearing up a little confusion regarding Mr Simkins here,' he replied, dismissing the subject. 'I'll take a quick look at Mr Fenn now, in the annexe. Then we'll proceed as usual. Dr Teasdell has been held up on Farnham Ward, by the way. She'll be along later.'

'Fine,' Rosemary replied, then hung back by Patti's side for a moment after the doctor had walked away, and spoke softly. 'Mr Simkins was up to his old tricks again, I gather.'

'If you mean lying to junior nurses who know no better?' Patti said bitterly.

'Yes, sorry. I meant to warn you but there was so much else to explain, I forgot. It's his little hobby, poor old thing. He's getting rather bored here. Dr Pritchard wasn't cross, was he?'

'Not very, I suppose, but I felt a bit embarrassed,' Patti confessed.

'I'll explain to him, shall I?'

'No. Thanks, but don't bother. It's not important.' Patti didn't want to let Angus think that she would get a more senior nurse to cover up or explain away any tiny mistake she made. She knew him well enough by now to be quite certain that that was not the kind of thing he admired.

'Okay, then. I'd better catch up with Dr Pritchard. He likes tea when he has finished. Do you think you could make it? One of the auxiliaries usually does it but they're busier on Mondays, so . . .'

'Of course. The tea will be there,' Patti assured her.

'Thanks.'

'Now, Mr Simkins, your temperature!'

Patti allowed a hint of ferocity into her tone and was rewarded by a very meek, 'Yes, Sister,' in reply. And this time she positively enjoyed the undeserved elevation of her status. Mr Simkins became slightly more animated a few minutes later as she was taking his pulse—probably trying to distract her into forgetting the count.

'He's a good doctor, that Pritchard fellow.'

'Is he?' Patti replied briefly.

'Yes. I mean, he's not my own doctor of course.' Mr Simkins was in for two rather difficult bowel operations, and this was not Angus Pritchard's speciality. 'But I've seen him at work enough these past three weeks.'

'Oh yes . . . ?' Twenty-six, twenty-seven, twenty-eight . . . The trouble was, she did want to hear this interesting new viewpoint on Angus. 'Just a minute. I have to count . . .' Thirty-two, thirty-three . . .

'He's friendly, but he's not familiar, if you know what I mean. He makes people believe he really does know how to cut 'em up, even if he doesn't.'

'Do you think he doesn't?' She had finished the count now and noted down the rate, so she could talk freely as she set up the sphygmomanometer to take a blood pressure reading.

'Oh no, Sister, I'm not saying that. I think he probably does know—mostly.'

Patti almost laughed aloud at this generous qualification.

'But what I mean is—' the old man continued '—well,

we're in a doctor's power while we're here, aren't we? Whether we like it or not.'

'I suppose so,' Patience conceded.

'So the more confidence we have in 'em, the better we feel. I mean, you can read stories in the papers these days telling you that doctors don't know a thing, and kill more people than they cure. I don't know if it's true, but when I see a story like that, I avoid it. I don't want to know. So what I'm really saying is a doctor like Pritchard, who has confidence in himself, like, is the best kind of doctor to have. He'll cure you psychosomastically, you see . . . Finished already?'

'I'm afraid so,' Patti laughed again. Psychosomastically indeed!

And after his tricky little attempt to avoid the procedure, the evident regret in his tone now that it was finished was rather comical. She guessed that, as Sister Watson had said, he was bored, or lonely perhaps, and would try to gain a nurse's attention even at the price of lying about the temperature and pulse routine.

Before washing her hands and moving to the next patient, Patti glanced quickly at the address recorded on Mr Simkins' card: Morgan Flats. She knew of the name by this time. It was a rather unattractive nearby development where a lot of older single people lived, and she guessed he was probably one of them. Now that the major part of his surgery was over and the prospect of returning home grew nearer, it was likely that Mr Simkins was coming to value contacts with people here that he could not enjoy in his little flat.

Patience Rainer was not the kind of nurse who needed to be reminded that patients are individual human beings and must be treated and understood as such, so it was almost subconsciously that she stored away these thoughts about Mr Simkins in her mind, ready for a time when such observations might be important. Now it was time to move on.

Just as she was finishing the round, Rosemary came through from the annexe area where she had been standing attentively at Dr Pritchard's side as he moved from bed to bed.

'The doctor will want his tea in a few minutes. How are you going?'

'Fine. This is the last one,' Pattie replied. 'Sandra helped me with a couple of things.'

'Yes, we're very lucky on this ward. All our auxiliaries are very capable. I'm sorry we couldn't do the annexe together as I said we would, but if you're not having any problems, that's great.'

She ducked out again and Patti packed away the equipment and went to the nurses' station to prepare the tea. Dr Pritchard and Sister Watson joined her there a few minutes later.

It was ridiculous, but preparing the doctor's tea had caused Patience more worry than anything else that whole morning. She somehow felt that he would judge her on it. If the brew was not to his taste, another black mark would go down against her in the conduct book he seemed to be keeping on her in his mind, whereas if he liked it . . . Would it soften him a little?

She ought not to care, and she told herself that she *didn't* care for personal reasons. It was simply that her career would suffer if this man's dislike was given a chance to grow. But the distinction between personal and professional feelings was a very artificial one. Where did your personal feelings begin and end when your profession was something as emotionally involving as nursing?

'I'll make it as strong as I like it, and leave hot water for him to add if he doesn't want it that way,' was her final conclusion.

He made no complaints however, merely reaching for the jug of milk, adding a few drops and settling back in his chair as though he would not get another chance to sit down for hours—which might well be the case, Patti thought, if he was going to Theatre after this.

'Pour yourself a cup and sit down too, Patti,' Rosemary said.

Patti complied, but with mixed feelings. She very much wanted a cup of tea and a short rest, but in the company of Dr Pritchard she did not know that she would feel very restful. And was he counting on her to refuse Sister Watson's invitation, after the agreement they had made six weeks ago that they would avoid being seen in each other's company? She noticed the quick glance he tossed her as she sat down in the one remaining chair, an uncomfortably stiff-backed one, which did not help her to relax.

'Enjoying your first morning on the ward, Nurse Rainer?' His question broke a short silence.

'Very much, thank you.'

'Of course, you've been doing only the most routine of tasks.' He was observing her narrowly as he spoke, as if this was some kind of test and he was waiting for her to fail it.

'But I've enjoyed it all the same. There's something satisfying about figures, recording them accurately and knowing that they will add up to a picture that can give a lot of information.' Patience stopped suddenly, feeling that she was in danger of running on too long in reply to what was merely a polite and meaningless question.

'I think your tan is starting to fade a little, Dr

Pritchard,' Rosemary put in, changing the subject as if she had sensed a tingle of tension in the air.

'Well, I've been back for three weeks now,' the surgeon replied. 'And there hasn't been much sun here to give it a boost.'

'Sunday was gorgeous though,' Patti put in rashly. 'I was home for the weekend and I had a wonderful ride through piles of dead leaves. My horse nearly went mad.'

'Oh, do you ride?' Rosemary asked with interest. Dr Pritchard made a reply on Patti's behalf.

'Yes, I'm afraid nursing is only Patience's second love, Sister Watson. She used to work as a stable-hand and we may find that the medical profession loses her to the equestrian life again one day.'

The words were delivered very smoothly, and Rosemary, at least, took them at face value. Patti was a little more wary.

'So you're only giving hospital life a trial, Patti?' Rosemary asked.

'Not at all,' Patience hastened to reply. 'Dr Pritchard is just teasing me.' She dared to look coldly at him.

'You two obviously know each other outside the hospital,' Rosemary said frankly, then her tone changed. 'Actually, yes, now I remember. I had heard . . .'

Patti coloured and she saw Angus pick up a pencil and tap it irritatedly and abstractedly against the surface of the desk next to him. Rosemary had obviously just made the connection between gossip heard in the staff dining-room and Patti's name. Evidently the story about her involvement with Angus had not died down completely even yet.

'Patience's parents are friends of mine,' Angus explained evenly, then he began to talk to Sister Watson about medical matters in a way that deliberately excluded Patti. She was not sorry, but sat back to finish her tea in peace, trying to listen and learn from what the two qualified people were saying.

Angus did most of the talking, explaining a particular method of care and post-operative treatment he wanted Rosemary to follow with a patient who would be returning from rather difficult surgery late that afternoon. Patti tried to concentrate on what he was saying, not on how he was saying it, but for some reason this was not easy.

She observed the intelligence and animation that transformed his features now that he was talking about something that interested him with someone he obviously liked. He was illustrating something with his hands now, making precise movements and shapes in the air with lean fingers that proclaimed his trade almost as surely as the white coat he wore.

His hands were tanned, too. Probably almost the whole of that long body would be a similar golden and faintly freckled brown, off-set in places by patches of darker hair.

Idly Patti noticed a few inches of the slim gold chain that threaded around his neck. Was that new? She did not remember having seen it that night when he had sat opposite her over coffee. It must have been a present from some lady-friend. Somehow, Patti did not think that Angus was a man who would deliberately go out and buy such a thing for himself. Perhaps it was Spanish gold, a holiday gift picked out from a market stall by the woman who had accompanied him during that sunny trip to Spain . . .

'Patti, we'll have to get on.' Rosemary interrupted

thoughts which had strayed much too far from where
they should have been.

'Good heavens, yes!' Patti exclaimed with a glance at
her watch. Rosemary laughed.

'It's not that bad. We are allowed a short break.
Would you take the linen lists down to the depot for me
before you get back to the ward? Carole or Sandra will
have them all made out. Just bring them for me to sign
first.'

Patti went in search of the lists while Rosemary turned
again to Dr Pritchard to receive a last instruction. He
had only just left when Patience returned to Rosemary
with the forms to be signed, so when she left the ward
herself she purposely slowed her steps.

'I'm sure he'll appreciate being allowed a clean get-
away,' she said to herself.

But to her surprise she saw that he had stopped near
one of the recessed cleaning bays and had turned in her
direction, obviously waiting for her to catch up. His face
was impassive, shadowed from the light on one side,
with the firm planes of his cheeks highlighted.

Patti approached him at a steady pace, uncertain
where to look. At the ground? At him? She solved the
problem by pretending to be earnestly consulting the
linen lists and was so intent on the little performance that
she almost overshot the mark and had to be pulled up by
a word from him.

'Patience!' He stepped into the recess and pulled her
after him just as an orderly walked past and glanced
curiously at the pair of them.

Dr Pritchard sighed as if thoroughly exasperated,
noticed the slightly open door of an adjacent store-room
used for cleaning equipment, and motioned her into it
ahead of him.

'Perhaps we can have a bit of privacy in here,' he said.

Patty looked around doubtfully. There was certainly no one else in the store-room, if room it could be called. There would scarcely have been enough space. The place was really no more than an oversized cupboard and Dr Pritchard was, of necessity, standing very close. Patience was aware that this was not as unpleasant a thing as it should have been.

'Is this a good idea?' she murmured. 'If someone tries to come in and sees us, they really will think there's something going on.'

Dr Pritchard's only response was to lock the door.

'This won't take long,' he said, running lean fingers through soft thick chestnut curls. 'I just wanted to find out how you're getting along with our little plan.'

'I presume you mean . . .' She hesitated, searching for the least embarrassing way of wording it.

'I mean I hope you have been seen to be having a full social life.' He pronounced the words with an intonation of light sarcasm.

'Dr Pritchard, I've been quite busy,' Patti replied. 'I have been studying, and I have spent several weekends with my parents. I can't just turn on an instant social life and dozens of boyfriends!'

'One would suffice. However, I do take your point,' he conceded, allowing her to observe at close range the delicious crinkling effect of his half-smile on the soft skin at the corners of his blue-green eyes.

No! She wasn't going to notice such things. Fortunately he became serious again almost immediately.

'I'm not going to insist, of course, but you must see how important it is now that you've been put on a ward where I have to be quite frequently. And you saw Sister

Watson's reaction just now. She had obviously heard the stories, so they haven't died yet.'

'Is it so important?' Patti sighed, only caring for the moment about getting out of this awkward situation.

He used the most delicious aftershave she had ever come across, and she could not help noticing the fine-grained texture of his skin just where the V of his collar bone made a hollow below his neck.

'To me it is important,' he said. 'You must see why. It would be different, perhaps, if we really were involved together. But I'm damned if I'm going to jeopardise my career or call into question my professional integrity because of some ridiculous rumour about myself and a junior nurse still in her teens.'

'I was twenty in April.'

'My apologies.'

'And what about you? Are you fulfilling your side of the bargain?' Patti was not yet quite ready to accept his arguments.

'Yes, I am, as it happens.'

She was unprepared for the quick sinking of her stomach that followed these words, and did not have time to wonder about what had caused it.

'Then I suppose I have no choice,' she said. 'If it is at all possible, I shall find myself at least one boy-friend. Perhaps I should advertise?' she finished bitingly.

'That won't be necessary, surely? You're really quite attractive.'

Was he laughing at her or with her? The former, probably.

'Are looks all that matter to you when you take someone out?' she asked coldly.

'No. But to some people they are. And I'm not

necessarily suggesting you should embark on anything serious.'

'Can't we stop this horrible conversation right now?' Patti pleaded, thoroughly weary.

'Yes, I know, it is horrible.' His tone had changed. 'Believe me, I feel as uncomfortable as you do, but unless you have any other suggestions, this is the way it has to be.'

It was the first time he had been completely serious and straightforward with her, and at this close range she suddenly realised that it was not only his appearance which was attractive. His voice, too, when he wanted it to be, could be mellow, sincere, and caressing.

Without realising what was happening, Patti relaxed the tense attitude she had been holding and this made her body sway closer to his. For a moment he continued to look down at her—quizzically now. She noticed the firmly moulded lines of his lips and wondered what it would be like to feel their pressure on hers. She would never know, of course . . .

Then he had turned to the door and reached a hand towards the lock, but the twisting movement he made produced no reaction, and when he tried the handle it would not turn.

'The lock's jammed,' he said shortly, breaking the disturbing mood.

'Oh no! That's just not possible!'

He turned back to her, their eyes met, and suddenly they both laughed, releasing a tension that had become unbearable. It was one of those rare times when for each the mood of the other person fuels the laughter, and they went on shaking with very surprising mirth for quite some time, trying to keep it as silent as possible.

'You *do* have a sense of humour!' Patti exclaimed,

before she could ask herself whether the remark was wise.

'Yes. I gather you find that surprising?' Angus answered.

'Well, it's surprising how many people haven't,' Patti countered.

'I'm glad I possess such a rare treasure then,' he said lightly. 'Now, the lock . . .'

'What are we going to do?'

'Don't worry. I know the locks in this hospital. They don't stay jammed forever. It's just a matter of a little . . . gentle . . . pressure—there!' He had been fiddling with the lock as he spoke, and as he had predicted it clicked and released quite easily.

'You go first,' he said. 'Or you'll be late with those lists.'

'Thanks.'

He pushed her gently towards the door, then reached an arm around and opened it, brushing her shoulders lightly with his hand as he did so. There was an instant in which he seemed to hesitate as if weighing up two courses of action, then quite deliberately he allowed his hand to rest against the firm square shape of her shoulder for a tiny but distinct moment.

'Good girl,' he said.

Patti did not dare to look back as she left the storeroom and hurried down the corridor. Was he watching her? No, he would have ducked back inside the confined space for a moment longer to allow her to continue on out of sight. Fortunately there appeared to be no one around, so it seemed that they were safe and had not been observed. Her heart was beating too fast.

'Much more than ninety a minute, I'm sure,' she said to herself.

And why? His brief touch? Or the laughter they had shared, which seemed for the first time to contain feelings of friendliness? It couldn't be that she was starting to be attracted to him when a few minutes ago she wouldn't even have been able to say that she liked him. One moment of laughter and warmth meant nothing at all . . .

CHAPTER FIVE

'HALLO, PATTI!' Mark Stewart greeted her that evening in the dining-hall as she walked past with her tray of food.

She returned his greeting, then on an impulse sat down at his table instead of going on to one of her regular spots by the window where she would have been joined soon by some of her special friends. Mark was one of the four young men who had started in the same batch of trainees as Patti herself, and she had already labelled him as 'probably nice' without as yet having tested this by getting to know him better.

'How was *your* first day? As uncomplicated as mine, I hope,' he said.

'I don't know. How uncomplicated was yours?' she returned lightly.

'Very. But I enjoyed it. I was a bit doubtful when I found out that I'd been put in Paediatrics,' Mark explained. 'I haven't had much to do with children before, and I was afraid they might take an instant dislike to me or something. But they didn't seem to.'

'Of course they didn't. You were underestimating yourself.'

'Thanks for your confidence. But what about you? You haven't answered my question properly yet.'

'Well, I had a good day too. I liked the Sister in charge of my ward, though of course we won't always be on the same shift. The Senior Sister, Hazel Gibson, seemed good too, although I only saw her a couple of times during the day.'

'No sticky encounters with irate surgeons?' Mark teased, but for Patti the light question struck a little too close to home. She wanted to keep this conversation away from subjects that reminded her in any way of Angus Pritchard.

'None whatsoever,' she managed to reply, lightly and untruthfully. 'Their visits passed off quite without incident.'

'I have a bit of a problem with doctors—male ones, anyway,' Mark confessed now. 'Most of them can't understand why I'm in a "women's profession" like nursing.'

'Why *did* you take it up?' Patti asked with gentle curiosity. 'It's still unusual. You and Thomas and Stephen and Robert must have felt rather conspicuous among the rest of us.'

'Sometimes we did, yes. I was tempted to do psychiatric nursing, simply because the split there between male and female nurses is roughly fifty-fifty, but I thought about it for a long time and I realised that that area just didn't interest me.'

'Mmm, it must have been a hard decision.'

'It was.'

There was a little silence, during which Patti looked up and watched some of the other staff passing the table with trays. Seconds later she wished she hadn't, because for once Dr Pritchard was eating here. He passed her table directly behind Mark's chair and tipped her an approving nod and half-wink as he glanced down and saw the male nurse leaning towards her to say something.

Patti acknowledged the surgeon's gesture with a nod,

an uncertain smile and a faint blush. There was no doubt that Dr Pritchard assumed this dinner-time conversation with Mark to be the first step in her promised campaign—was that the right word?—to deflect attention from the supposed relationship between their two selves. The whole thing was so embarrassing.

Mark had noticed Patti's smile and followed her gaze, catching sight of Dr Pritchard as he threaded his way between the next two tables.

'That's Angus Pritchard, isn't it? The micro-surgeon?'

'Yes,' Patti replied briefly.

'That's right, you know him, don't you? In fact, you're going out with him. Or is that just a rumour?'

'Just a rumour, and absolutely untrue,' Patti replied spiritedly, seizing on this opportunity to deny the story to someone she sensed would believe her—although she had told other people in whom she had the same confidence and it didn't seem to have done much good. Far too many people were still asking her the same question that Mark just had.

'It's terrible here sometimes, isn't it?' Mark said. 'I suppose any work environment is the same. Sometimes it's just friendly interest, and at others it's harmful gossip.'

'I agree absolutely,' Patti replied. 'I do know Dr Pritchard, of course. The rumours didn't start from nothing at all. My parents are friends of his. In fact my father is his godfather. But apart from meeting him several times when I was a child, I feel I hardly know the man.'

After this, the subject of conversation drifted away from Angus Pritchard again, and the two students sat quite happily over their meal. Patti wasn't surprised, when the talk shifted to films, that Mark suggested they see one together later that week. She agreed to the idea with no hesitation, then wondered whether it had been right to do so.

What she knew of Mark Stewart she liked—he reminded her of her brother Timothy. But was she accepting his invitation because she liked him, or because of what she had promised to Dr Pritchard earlier that day? But perhaps it didn't matter whichever it was, and she was becoming stupidly over-sensitive to the whole issue.

'Which film?' she said, putting enthusiasm into her tone.

'It's up to you. There are about three I'd like to see that are on fairly near.'

He named three films which didn't particularly appeal to Patti, but she picked the one that most suited her own taste and he looked quite pleased.

'I do have a car though, if you'd like to go further afield. We could check the paper and see what's on?'

'No, what we've decided is fine,' Patti hastened to say, and they parted company, having agreed that Wednesday would be the best day as they would be less tired after a spell in the training centre than on the ward.

'Spurning our company this evening, Patience Rainer!' Lisa said, coming up and linking her arm through Patti's as the latter was walking out of the dining-hall.

'I was too tired to get as far as our usual table,' she joked in reply.

'You were talking to Mark Stewart,' plump but pretty Janice said. 'He's nice, isn't he?'

'Yes. I only began to get to know him tonight, but we're going to see a film on Wednesday, so . . .'

'Good for you!' Lisa said. Patti could see that she would have liked to have probed a little deeper, but was too tactful. Perhaps when they were alone, Lisa would ask if there are anything serious in it.

'What about tonight?' Lisa was saying now. 'Shall we do something? Go for coffee and a good talk?'

'Not late, because we'll all on A shifts tomorrow,' Janice reminded her.

'It would be good though,' Patti agreed. 'We don't want to get into the habit of parking ourselves down in front of the television every night just because we've been working.'

'It's settled then,' Lisa announced. 'I'm going to change first though, because I want to take you to a place I discovered at the weekend, and it's a little more up-market than our usual. Is that all right? And shall we ask Celine too?'

The other two girls agreed to both proposals. Celine was a petite French dietician whom Lisa had recently befriended and with whom she made rather hilarious attempts to practise her very schoolgirl French.

The party of four girls assembled at the arranged rendezvous in the foyer, ready to leave, half an hour later. They had all changed into clothes that were pretty and fashionable but not too dressy. Patti wore a peasant-style skirt and top in a rich dark red that was almost rust in some lights and which brought out the pink of her cheeks and heightened the blonde delicacy of her hair.

'We mustn't walk or sit together,' Lisa joked, refer-ring to the fact that her own pullover and skirt in a clear muted pink clashed rather horribly with Patti's colours.

Nevertheless they did walk together, as Lisa led the

way and the other two dropped behind a little. Patti could hear the dark-haired and Gallic-featured Celine entertaining Janice with stories of her home town of Lyon in English that had already increased its fluency markedly since her arrival.

'Ought we to slow down so they can keep up?' Patti suggested.

'I don't think they mind,' Lisa replied. 'And I'm happy to talk just with you. Tell me more about Mark Stewart—unless you think I'm prying horribly.'

'I don't think you're prying,' Patti returned. 'But really there's nothing to tell. We were talking about movies and he asked if I'd like to see one with him, that's all.'

'So this isn't the fulfilment of a secret dream you've been cherishing for weeks?' Lisa probed lightly.

'No, I'm afraid not. Sorry to disappoint you.'

'I'm not disappointed. If you had said it was, I would have thought privately that you weren't quite right for each other.'

'Really?'

'No discredit to him, and of course it's only a superficial judgment, but I think he's too dreamy. He's aiming for a very quiet life, a little cottage somewhere, part-time nursing and herb-gardening for a little extra money.'

'Herb-gardening? He told you all this?'

'Yes. Medicinal herbs. We did that group project together a few weeks ago, the one on community nursing, and had quite a few good chats then.'

'And you, little matchmaker, noted down everything he said so that you'd be able to advise your friends whether he was suited to them or not!' Patience exclaimed in mock indignation.

'Exactly,' Lisa replied complacently. 'A very necessary role, believe me. So many girls just will not see what's good for them.' She lowered her voice a little and went on. 'Now, *I* think Mark Stewart would be a better prospect for our Janice, don't you?'

'Janice!'

'Yes. She's a country girl at heart, with those cheerful milkmaid looks of hers.'

'Milkmaid looks! Lisa! I had no idea you went into all this so deeply!'

'Our friendship is yet young, dear. All the sinister depths of my personality are not revealed at once. But don't start thinking I'm like that dreadful Alison Reed. I only gossip and matchmake in the nicest possible way, because I enjoy seeing people happy—being so happy myself with John,' Lisa added, speaking about her steady boyfriend of two years, who was a junior banker in the City.

'All right, I accept your justification,' Patti conceded, never having doubted Lisa's motives for a moment. There were two ways to conduct this kind of conversation, and Lisa's was the nice kind. 'But what do you mean "country girl"? I consider myself a country girl, you know.'

'No, you're an outdoor girl. There's a difference. Janice's favourite country animals are hens and chickens. Yours are horses. Janice and Mark—hypothetically speaking, of course—will have a lovely farm together, very small, and will be perfectly happy. But you need vast acres, or else no acres at all but a chance to fulfil all those ambitions you were telling me about the other day. Rock-climbing, and trekking through Canada on horseback, and sailing on the Mediterranean.'

'Those are secret ambitions, remember,' Patti

warned, thinking back to an evening of lazy confidences they had had recently in which she had sketched out some of her wilder fantasies about future holidays. 'I'll probably never do half of them.'

'Yes, you will,' Lisa insisted. 'And you'll do them with some wonderful athletic man, too. Angus Pritchard is your type, I think.'

'Oh no, Lisa, not you too!' Patti groaned.

The two girls had almost completely avoided the sensitive subject up until now. Lisa had asked, of course, how it was that she was acquainted with him, but had never teased or even spoken about the rumours that they were secretly involved together. She brought it up now for the first time.

'Why not? I know there's nothing in those ridiculous stories that you're going out together now, but I don't see why it shouldn't happen one day.'

'*I* do! I can't stand the man!' Patti retorted a little too strongly.

'Can't you? I'm embarrassed to admit this in view of the way our dear Alison carries on, but he does have a certain claim to divine good looks.'

'Looks aren't everything.' Patti gave this opinion for the second time that day, thinking that it already seemed a long time since she had stood in the cramped space of the cleaning store-room with the much-talked-about surgeon—an occurrence not even Lisa would hear about.

'Of course they're not!' Lisa was agreeing. 'But he's got a lot more going for him than just looks.'

'Yes! Arrogance, conceit, pomposity . . .'

'Rubbish! It's the dignity of his position. We're only first-year students, remember. Everyone seems arrogant and pompous to me until I remind myself of that.

But listen, Dr Pritchard is active and sporty like you. He rides . . .'

'Does he? I don't think so,' Patti said.

'He does. I overheard him talking about it to someone. I'm surprised he hasn't told you, since he must know that you do.'

'Yes . . .'

Patti was surprised too, and somehow a little hurt. If Angus Pritchard had not even bothered to tell her that they shared an interest in common, he must dislike her more than she had thought—and much more than the episode this morning would have led her to believe.

The other two girls caught up to Lisa and Patience at that moment, so the tête-à-tête could not continue. Lisa addressed a question to Celine, Janice listened in to the French girl's reply and Patti was glad to find that she was left to her own thoughts for a few moments.

Why was she suddenly so disappointed and depressed? She had just told Lisa in very vehement terms that she did not like the chestnut-haired micro-surgeon at all, and now she was acting as though finding that he felt the same was a terrible blow. Well, it is never pleasant to find out for certain that you are not liked, she reflected, trying to make herself believe that this wound to the ego was the only thing that was hurting.

But really there was something more, and she knew it. When Lisa had said that the two of them had things in common and had put Angus's lofty manner down to his professional status, instead of agreeing that it was an innate and unpleasant trait of character as Patti had suggested, she had felt pleased.

There was no use in denying it any longer. She was becoming terribly attracted to the man. It meant nothing, of course. It was purely physical—her wretched hormones, or something, she thought, remembering the chapter of a textbook she had recently read entitled *Endocrine Responses in the Human Organism*. But the whole thing was a nuisance, as she would have to spend time and effort getting over it.

I keep telling people that looks don't count, she said to herself fiercely, and now I've gone all silly about Angus Pritchard just because he's gorgeous.

There was no other reason. His looks, his voice, the indefinable combination of subtle scents that hovered about him . . . On one level—a physical one—she could be seduced into an attraction by these things, but it would go no further.

It had taken a surprisingly long time to work through these thoughts, and when she began to concentrate on where she was going once more. Patti found that they were walking along a street that seemed faintly familiar.

'Have I been here before?' she spoke the thought aloud. 'I feel as though I have.'

'You might have,' Lisa replied. 'The place I'm taking you to is on Welland Road. I'm sorry it's such a walk, but John and I enjoyed it so much when we had supper here . . .'

'We don't mind,' Celine assured her. 'Me, I'm glad of the fresh air, after so much hospital smells all day.'

They turned into Welland Road at that moment and ahead Patti recognised the lights of the coffee house where she had been for the disastrously short outing with Dr Pritchard two months ago.

'This is the place just here,' Lisa said. 'It's called the Coffee-Pot. Not a very original name . . . *Have* you been here, Patti?'

'No, I'm getting mixed up, I think,' Patti replied hastily. 'I have a very bad sense of direction at night.'

The white lie easily deflected Lisa's curiosity and Patti's awkwardness went unnoticed by her three companions. It was ridiculous to be feeling awkward anyway. The fact that Dr Pritchard knew of this place didn't mean he would be here tonight. He was probably still on duty. And even if chance did play one of its tricks and he walked in, their pact reinforced only that day would ensure that he did not speak to her. In fact, ironically, she was now in a perfect position to weather out the storm of her stupid attraction.

The Coffee-Pot was a much nicer place than she had remembered. After all, the last time she had been here she had not really had the time or opportunity to have many memories of it at all! The four tired hospital workers chose a quiet corner and ordered hot chocolate, tempting each other into choosing a big piece of gooey and delicious cake each as well.

It was a frivolous evening of talk about their work, their lives at home, their plans for the future. Patti enjoyed it after she had deliberately made herself choose a seat which faced the wall rather than out into the room. She was not going to look up every time someone came in, hoping—or dreading—that it would be Angus Pritchard!

Nevertheless, after they had sat for a good long while over their supper and indeed he hadn't come, she was conscious, and annoyed, that she felt vaguely disappointed.

Back at the nurses' home her room seemed lonely for once. Mostly the presence of dozens of other nurses above, below and on either side, indicated by faint noises—a laugh, footsteps, the sound of a door closing—

was enough to remind Patti of the companionship and stimulation to be found in hospital life, but not tonight.

'I'm just tired after my first day,' she said to herself aloud as she undressed.

A long silky night-gown of pale apricot, cool fresh sheets and warm fluffy blankets provided comfort, and she must have been tired because it was only a few minutes before she was asleep.

The next morning at breakfast, Mark Stewart sought her out to suggest that after all they make the outing for Friday night.

'There's a five-fifteen session of the film,' he said. 'Since we're not working the next day we could see that, then have dinner somewhere afterwards—or is that too heavy an evening for you?'

'No, no, that's all right,' Patti hastened to agree, noticing how anxious to please he seemed. 'Not somewhere too formal though.'

'I agree,' Mark nodded. 'We'll find a place near the cinema. Indian or Italian or something.'

This change of arrangements left the remaining three evenings of the week clear and Patti was glad of it. Nursing was by no means light work. She felt tired physically, mentally and emotionally at the end of each day, though of course she would get used to it.

By the end of the week this was beginning to happen. The routine of working in A shift with its early start was becoming less of a shock to the system, though the same could not yet be said of the jolt suffered by all her internal organs each time Dr Pritchard walked on to the ward!

Bed-making, as Patience had feared, took more of her

energy than it should. And three times it had been Dr Pritchard who had come across her struggling red-faced with a recalcitrant draw-sheet, or kicking wheels which for everyone else seemed to move with oiled smoothness. Each time he had simply raised a well-drawn eyebrow, twitched a facial muscle into what may have been a faint smile, murmured, 'Carry on, Nurse,' and continued past her with assertive footsteps to his patient further down the ward.

Patience began to wonder whether he had some kind of sixth sense that told him whenever she was about to do something particularly clumsy. Normally—apart from the dreaded beds and even they were quickly getting better—her work was neat and smooth.

It was good enough to draw praise from Nicola Barrett, the Sister who worked two morning shifts on Rosemary Watson's days off, and who was rather less friendly than the St Lucian Sister Patti had warmed to so much on her first day. But as soon as Angus Pritchard came along, Patti's fingers suddenly lost all coordination. On Friday morning Patti counted up the incidents that had occurred. Not including struggling with beds, there were still four.

On Tuesday, when she had been helping Sandra with the patients' morning tea, she had picked up a packet of biscuits that turned out to be open at both ends and seventeen ginger-snaps had cascaded on to a surprised patient's bed. On Thursday a piece of rubber tubing had sprung out of her hand like a catapult and winged its way across the ward annexe.

Later that morning Angus had been walking past the sluice room just as Patti accidentally unscrewed some kind of special valve from one of the taps—to be rewarded by a fine jet of water spray directly in her face.

Sister Barrett had leant over immediately and shut it off, but Patti was quite sure that Dr Pritchard had witnessed at least part of the occurrence.

This morning's incident had been the last straw. She had been at Angus's side and he had asked for a cotton ball. Absolutely determined that she should demonstrate an irreproachable piece of nursing, she had picked it up nimbly with a pair of dressing forceps and opened them to let the tuft of cotton wool drop into his hand.

Unfortunately it did not, having become hooked to the square-cornered ends. She shook the forceps. The cotton refused to let go. She shook again. Finally the surgeon himself detached it with an impatient tweak of his gloved hand and went back to his delicate work.

Patti realised that she had forgotten to include Monday morning's piece of juggling with the patients' record cards in her list. That, plus the beds, plus the other four slapstick incidents . . . Eight times in four days that she had humiliated herself in front of the man whose admiration—grudging at first perhaps, but then warm and unqualified—she most wanted.

Looking back over the week on Friday afternoon, she decided that it was Dr Pritchard's presence on the ward that had exhausted her more than anything else.

Since Mark was not meeting her with his tiny secondhand car in front of the nurses' home until a quarter to five, and the A shift finished at three, Patti decided she had time for a much-needed hour lying down before getting ready. This left her far more refreshed and looking forward to the prospect of the evening than she had expected to be. After an invigorating shower she decided to wear something a little more dressy than she had intended.

The outfit was dark blue, dotted with white and made of a chiffon-like fabric that billowed out above the matching underskirt. It was a summer or spring dress really, with its wide, white-trimmed rounded neckline and elbow sleeves, but a coat would keep out the chill of the November air.

Patti's one fear was that the style was too childish. She had not forgotten Alison Reed's light but barbed comment that she was pretty apart from looking so young, and had wondered several times since, as she assessed her appearance in the mirror, if there was any truth in it. Angus Pritchard had thought that she was still in her teens, too. Patti even confided her fears to Lisa one evening.

'Rubbish!' had been Lisa's comment on this idea. 'You look fabulous sometimes. Just like that gorgeous American actress. What's her name? She played a nurse in a film quite recently, I'm sure. Jessica something-or-other. I get positively envious of you.'

Patti had assessed Lisa's fine-boned, dark-haired prettiness, then her own appearance in the mirror, and decided that Lisa's words were flattery made out of kindness rather than envy on Lisa's part. But the reassurance had quieted her doubts a little.

Now she felt them again and attempted to do something about it, spending quite some time arranging her hair in a more formal variation of her usual nurse's knot, with wispy gossamer tendrils framing her face in a halo that gave it greater softness. Bright silver earrings, a bracelet and necklace completed the picture, as well as a light touch of make-up, which was all her clear young skin and large sapphire eyes needed.

At twenty to five she was satisfied and hurried down to meet Mark. His reaction was gratifying, if slightly awkwardly expressed.

'I should have dressed up more. You look great.'

'Thanks,' she replied, adding, 'but you're fine, too, in any case.'

Mark wore dark pants, a beige shirt and a tweed jacket that added maturity to his wiry build. He was by no means a companion to be ashamed of, but Patti still felt a little embarrassed, wondering whether she would have accepted his invitation so easily if Angus Pritchard hadn't been in the picture. Was he similarly occupied tonight? Apart from that one cool comment of his on Monday, she knew nothing about his relationships with women.

'You're very thoughtful,' Mark was saying. They had climbed into his modest little car and were already on their way. 'Problem on the ward?'

'Oh . . . not really.' Patti recalled her thoughts, realised she was being rude and manufactured a story. 'We have a rather sweet old man I'm a bit worried about, even though I thought I was going to loathe him on the first day. I suppose I oughtn't to tell you his name, or is that carrying ethics a bit far?'

'Perhaps a bit far, since I'm staff too. It depends what you're going to tell me.'

'It's nothing really. I just have the feeling that, even though he gives us a bit of trouble sometimes, when the time comes we're going to have difficulty sending him home.'

'How come? What does he say?' Mark queried.

'It's not what he says . . . I can't explain. I've just put two and two together. Little things. I think he's very lonely.'

'That kind of thing happens quite often, I dare say, once people are convalescent and have forgotten the immediate shock of being operated on. If they don't have much to go home to, hospital can seem quite a friendly place. But what can you do?'

Nothing, of course. I mean, at the end of next week or whenever Dr Teasdell decides, he'll just have to go because we need the beds, but . . .'

'The hospital social worker might put him into some kind of community scheme where he can get the same kind of companionship,' Mark suggested, and Patti agreed.

They talked shop of this kind for a while longer, then turned down a side-street and squeezed into a minute parking space.

'You see, it's not that I can't afford a bigger car,' Mark assured Patience solemnly. 'It's that I prefer the convenience of easy parking.'

Patti enjoyed the lightweight French film more than she had expected to, and Mark was good company in the limited way that anyone can be good company during a film. They had already picked out a quiet and not too expensive-looking Italian restaurant on their way down the main street before parking the car, and Mark had walked up to book a table before the film started, so after they emerged from the cinema at a quarter to eight they made their way straight there.

'I got a table near the window,' Mark said. 'I hope that's all right with you. It's interesting to watch people coming in and going past, don't you think?'

'Yes, I do, so I don't mind at all,' Patti replied.

'It's funny, I hadn't actually heard of this place, but when I saw the name today I realised it's one that I've heard some of the staff say is very good.'

'And it's on a fairly direct route between Ricky's and the West End,' Patti added. 'People might come here for a meal before going on to a show or a disco.'

As if in confirmation of this, the door opened at that moment and two very well-dressed people entered, obviously intending to go on somewhere afterwards. Patti noticed and admired the woman first. She had a sophisticated sweep of rich auburn hair that owed some of its burgundy lights to tinting rather than nature, but the effect was so striking that this did not matter. She wore a gold tunic-style top, figure-hugging pants of black Lycra, and a sparkling array of jewellery.

All this Patti took in after only a few seconds. The woman's companion still had his back to Patti's table as he spoke to the waiter about their reservation. As soon as he began to turn in her direction, Patti realised that the familiarity of the set of his shoulders and of the curls of dark chestnut hair against his collar was not just coincidence.

A minute ago she would have thought that fate really was singling her out for unfair treatment, but Mark's comment about the restaurant being known to hospital staff had already half-prepared her . . .

Angus Pritchard was looking directly at her now. Their eyes met for a long moment, then she saw the corners of his mouth lift into the hint of an approving smile as he registered Mark's presence. The ruby-haired woman at his side turned and touched him on the forearm, trailing her fingers in a brief, relaxed caress against the soft sleeve of his dark suede jacket. The pair moved away into a dim corner of the restaurant where, annoyingly, they were still just within view of Patti's gaze.

Mark was trying to turn around far enough to see who

had come in without his movement and curiosity seeming too obvious.

'Someone from the hospital?' he asked.

'Dr Pritchard, and a friend who I don't know,' Patti replied briefly. 'Shall we look at the menu?'

They consulted it together and each chose a light entrée followed by a main dish of pasta, but Patti was aware that her mind was not fully focused where it should be. If only Angus hadn't come in, because she doubted that she would be able to stop thinking about him now, and that was unfair to Mark.

Patti was feeling much too curious about the woman Angus was with, too. They made a very, *very* attractive couple, and were obviously on their way to somewhere special tonight—an ultra-smart disco in the West End, no doubt, judging by Angus's modern yet immaculate clothes. He wore the suede jacket, a cream silk shirt, dark pants, and the familiar gold chain round his neck, and complemented his glittering companion perfectly.

It was difficult to believe that the lovely woman was simply someone Angus had picked up in order to scotch hospital rumours. She was probably much more special to him than that—perhaps she had accompanied him to Spain. It was very probable, judging by her skin, still tanned a faint golden brown. Or was that just the impression created by skilful make-up in the dim yellow light of the restaurant?

Mark cleared up part of the mystery after the waiter had come to take their order.

'I got a little look at Dr Pritchard's friend,' he said. 'I've seen her before. I think she's some kind of actress, but I wouldn't know her name. Anyway, it's not really our business.'

No, it wasn't their business—but an actress! Patti

thought. What hope did she have then, a mere student nurse? But no, this wasn't the way to think. Was she really beginning to hope that Angus would return the attraction that she was fighting within herself? Of course not.

Angus Pritchard was as disturbed and annoyed by Patience's presence in the restaurant as she was by his. She had been on his mind far too much this week.

At first he hadn't minded in particular that she had been placed on a ward where he spent quite a bit of time, but Sister Watson's embarrassed reference to the rumours that had been going round had worried him. Then that awkard little encounter in the store-room had cleared things up between them, but Patti hadn't disappeared from his thoughts after this as she should have done.

And it had definitely not been part of his plan that her lively, wayward prettiness should suddenly force itself on his notice. It was that first morning on the ward. Up until then he had been able to think of her as the child he still felt she was, but the sight of her, pink-cheeked and flustered as she stood looking at that ridiculous sheaf of cards fanned out on the floor, with two fly-away wisps of blonde hair escaping from her cap and framing her face with brightness on either side, brought to him the knowledge that she would soon make a distractingly lovely woman.

He reminded himself in vain of his initial judgment of her character—frivolous, shallow, grasping, naive. Since then he had been continually looking for evidence of these things, and at times thought he had found them. But could he have been mistaken all along?

But no, why did he suddenly want to think this? All

right, perhaps he could concede that he liked her in many ways. There was nothing wrong with that. It was the same kind of feeling one might have for a much younger cousin, he told himself . . .

Then he thought of the other times he had seen her on the ward this week, and for a moment struggled to suppress laughter which Marianne would have thought the height of rudeness—and she would have been right, of course.

But pictures of the young nurse with her slim body— sometimes it seemed to contain that endearing mixture of grace and gawkiness which young horses have— remained in his mind. Her feet kicking those silly little wheels on the big hospital beds, her comical expression of silent rage and disbelief as she followed with her gaze the trajectory of the rubber tubing across the room, her blushing embarrassment as she made that impotent gesture with the forceps, trying to shake off the cotton bud. Angus had very much wanted to burst out laughing then, but was terrified about what it might do to this professional dignity in front of several patients and a first-year nurse, so he had been forced to adopt an unrealistically grim expression.

Angus wanted to look across at Patience now and smile, but she would think it strange after all his insist-ence on avoiding and ignoring each other. She had certainly taken him at his word about picking up an instant boyfriend, he reflected, frowning . . .

'What's wrong, darling? You're very silent tonight,' Marianne said, breaking in on thoughts which were, it was true, too exclusive of his dinner partner.

'Nothing,' he replied, trying to be offhand. 'Problems at the hospital. They're confidential and not really im-portant enough to waste my time over anyway. I'll put them out of my mind right now.'

'Good, because I've finished my Brandy Alexander, so we really must look at the menu. I can see the waiter hovering over there.'

Angus took the wine list and studied it, taking a long time over his choice because again he was not really concentrating. He had glimpsed Patti in her window-side corner, her finely-formed chin cupped in a hand whose fingers were already slightly pink-tipped from the rigours of nursing.

Light shone from behind her and from one side, turning her fine hair to spun gold and making touches of silver at her ears, wrists and throat sparkle. Tonight she looked much more mature than her twenty years—too old for the boy sitting opposite her, who must still be in his teens. Although, Angus reflected, she seemed serene and happy in his company.

He glanced up at her again. Yes, look. Now she was chatting to him and they both seemed quite animated. Angus and Marianne were usually livelier themselves, though lately the relationship seemed to have reached an awkward point. Angus wasn't quite sure where it should go next. Perhaps he should have invited her to Spain with him as he had at one time thought of doing. It might have cemented things between them and allowed him to become a little more sure of what they were looking for together.

'The wine waiter is here,' Marianne jogged his elbow gently.

'Er . . . sorry. We'll have a bottle of the . . . claret,' he said, making the choice on the spur of the moment.

'A very discerning selection, sir,' the waiter murmured, just as Angus registered the fact that he had chosen one of the most expensive wines on a by no

means cheap list. Unless he could pull himself together
quite quickly, this was not going to be a very successful
evening . . .

CHAPTER SIX

PATIENCE slept in the next morning, luxuriously and unashamedly, until half-past nine. The evening with Mark had turned out pleasantly, but no more than that. After a resolute and largely successful attempt to shut Dr Pritchard out of her thoughts, she had managed to keep up a flow of conversation with Mark, although they did not turn out to have much in common other than their interest in nursing and the world of medicine.

They left the restaurant at half-past nine and Mark did not suggest that they go anywhere else. Patti suspected that he would decide, as she had, that casual friendship would be the best thing to happen between them.

She had been very aware as she left the restaurant that Dr Pritchard and his lovely companion were still eating, having progressed at a very relaxed pace through their entrée and now enjoying a rich main course of seafood. It was evident that they were planning to have a very late night, and Patti presumed that Dr Pritchard was not working today.

The weekend was one of the quietest she had spent at Ricky's and by Sunday morning she was feeling a little depressed. Lisa had gone away with her boyfriend John and his family, Janice had visits from two old school-friends, and most of the other nurses with whom Patti got on well seemed to have gone to their permanent homes or to stay with friends.

Patti reflected that she ought to have done the same. Instead she would be at her parents' next weekend, which no doubt would turn out to be a much livelier one socially. In fact she already knew of two parties that were on.

She ended up spending most of Sunday lying in her room reading a paperback novel—as well as, it must be confessed, staring at the ceiling thinking very unproductive thoughts about Angus Pritchard.

It was a relief when Monday morning came, even though she doubted she would ever get used to the garish rattle of the alarm jolting her out of sleep at six when at this time of the year it was still pitch dark.

This week was a better one on the ward. Sister Barrett was on an afternoon, or B shift, as it was universally called, while Rosemary Watson, with whom Patti got on much better was working As every day. Patti was surprised at how quickly and readily she learned to handle all the routine tasks of the ward and was gratified that Rosemary rewarded each demonstration of keenness and ability by showing her how to perform a more complicated procedure. Rosemary even allowed her to tackle dressings, for which Patti showed a surprising aptitude, as long as Angus Pritchard was not nearby to turn her slim fingers to jelly.

Patti learned to distinguish which patients would belong to which surgeon. Dr Teasdell, a middle-aged and rather hearty but very pleasant woman, dealt with most of the digestive tract surgery—removal of gallstones and appendixes, for example, and three more doctors came and went fairly regularly. Dr Pritchard's patients were those who had had or were about to have plastic surgery. This was not face-lifts or other kinds of luxury cosmetic surgery as Patti had hazily assumed before she began nursing, but vital reconstructive work on injuries and displacements caused by accidents and burns.

Through remarks here and there from Rosemary, Patti discovered that Angus Pritchard was heavily involved in one of the newest branches of micro-surgery, the re-attachment of severed parts of the body, and would be called to assist in or observe operations of this kind at other hospitals nearby, as well as at the Sir Richard Gregory Memorial.

'Isn't he rather young to be so involved in such a particular field?' Patti asked one day when the subject had come up while she was working in the nurses' station with Rosemary.

'Yes, he is,' Rosemary agreed. 'But apparently he decided very early on in his training that that was the area he wanted to work in, and he has been pretty single-minded about it ever since. When I first came to Ricky's it took me ten months before I worked out who he was because he was away so much working with other people and doing research towards his Fellowship. It's probably part of the reason he's not married yet. He hasn't stayed still long enough until recently for any woman to make any headway with him at all!'

'What do you mean "till recently"?' Patti queried, treading the borderline between normal curiosity and unnatural eagerness to hear more about the chestnut-haired surgeon.

'Well, it's only this year that he has been permanently based at this hospital,' Rosemary explained, adding cheerfully, 'so I've no doubt that there are a dozen girls here who are pining after him.'

Patti grew hot and concentrated carefully on sorting through the new supplies she was cataloguing. Rosemary was right! This stupid infatuation for Angus was nothing special. Going weak at the knees when he walked on to the ward meant nothing at all. She was just one among a dozen, and there was about as much chance of the feeling becoming something more real as there was of her marrying a . . . an Albanian prince! She would change the topic of conversation now before it got altogether too dangerous.

'What about you, Rosemary. Do you have any further ambitions? Are you going to specialise in a definite area?'

'Probably,' replied the Sister. 'In fact I've almost definitely decided to go to Scotland half-way through next year to do midwifery.'

'Why Scotland?' Patti was curious.

'I feel like a change. I've lived in this area of London ever since I was two years old. I couldn't do midder at Ricky's, so I might as well make a big break and go somewhere a long way away . . . Besides,' she added with a mischievous smile, 'I met a nice Scottish physiotherapist in the summer and we've been writing ever since.'

'Aha! So that's it,' Patti laughed.

Through conversations such as this, as well as their work together on the ward, the two girls quickly developed quite a firm friendship, and as the weeks passed, Patti found that she loved the work of nursing more and more. Old Mr Simkins, the first patient with whom Patti felt she had had real human contact, went home eventually, obviously a little desolated at the prospect but looking forward to occasional visits to the Outpatients section of the hospital and planning to join a nearby senior citizens' club whose address had been given to him by the hospital social worker.

'I've never fancied the idea of such a place before,' Mr Simkins had said to Patti when telling her about it. 'But Jack Ridley who was next to me in bed for ten days, he said he goes along and it's not too bad. So I'll give it a go and see what happens.'

Other patients had taken his place since, of course, forming a kaleidoscope of different impressions for Patti, who had never come across such a wide range of people before. Again, she spoke about this to Rosemary, who agreed that people were the single most fascinating thing about nursing.

'Which is as it should be,' she added. 'If you're not interested in all kinds of people, you might as well find yourself a career somewhere else.'

It was evident that Alison Reed must have come to a similar conclusion, because one day just before Christmas Patti met her carrying two heavy suitcases through the foyer of the nurses' home.

'I've chucked it!' the dark-haired girl announced in response to Patti's questioning glance. 'This life just isn't for me, I'm afraid. I still go green at the sight of blood, even though they said I wouldn't after the first week or so. And I'm sick of having to keep up a cheerful expression in front of a lot of boring old moaners. We've only had one interesting patient in six weeks—a racing driver with hyperbaric oxygenation.'

'With hyperbaric what?' Patti asked incredulously.

'Or, well, actually no. I think that was part of the treatment we gave him. Or it might have been someone else who had that. I can't remember. Anyway, he went home two weeks ago. *And* he was married.'

'So what are you going to do now?' Patti asked.

'I've found a flat in a much better area with two girlfriends. I'm going to do temping for a while—I've got typing—then some kind of course in something else. Perhaps beauty therapy. I think I'll meet more interesting people that way. See you around, anyway—and good luck with your conquest of what's-his-name.'

'Goodbye, Alison, and good luck with everything,' Patti said, not trying very hard to be sincere. It was typical that the last thing Alison Reed would probably ever say to her should be on the tender subject of Angus Pritchard.

Patti's relationship with the disturbingly attractive surgeon continued in an uneasy equilibrium. Her bed-making skill had increased markedly so she no longer felt humiliated on that score, and the nightmare scenario of dropping a full bedpan at his feet had not yet been translated into reality, but nevertheless she rarely, if ever, felt at ease in his company.

And yet the unwilling attraction he had aroused in her would not go away.

A week before Christmas Glenn Baker was put in Jackson Ward one afternoon when Patti was working a B shift. He had already spent many weeks in the special burns unit at the hospital after a car accident that had left him with not simply the heat burns from the flaming petrol that had splattered him, but acid burns from the car battery as well.

Bad scarring was the result of all this, as well as permanent but minor loss of movement in his left arm, and now, after going home for a final convalescence, he was back at Ricky's for extensive plastic surgery. As Patti took care of all the necessary admission procedures she could see that her new patient was nervous about the idea of surgery and she could not blame him. From the details on his record card, it appeared that he was thirty years old and comparatively well off and successful in his career in management and public relations in a branch of the travel industry. The painful experience of severe burning and the long process of recovery was almost certainly the worst thing that had ever happened to him, and understandably the idea of another spell in hospital filled him with dread.

'I wish we didn't have to come in the night before,' he joked as Patti wrote down the last of the admission details. 'I wish they could knock you out with a quick shot at home, whisk you into Theatre, do their stuff and pop you into Recovery before you even realised anything was going on.'

'This won't be as bad as before,' Patti promised truthfully with a smile.

'I hope not, Nurse, I tell you. There were a few days when I would have died to escape that pain, even with drugs. Now I'm glad I didn't die, but if I thought I'd be going through it again, I'd . . . I don't know what I'd do.'

'Yes, burns are painful,' Patti replied inadequately.

What she knew about the pain of burns and the discomfort of plastic surgery came only from her reading, so she didn't know quite how much reassurance she should give.

But she did feel a particular interest in this patient— *not* because Angus Pritchard would be his doctor, she insisted to herself. It was the most dramatic case of burn scarring she had yet come across, and she guessed that before the traumatic accident and the initial grafting that had followed, Glenn Baker would have been very good-looking indeed.

How much could even Dr Pritchard's skilled hands do? Glenn Baker had come in alone, but that evening his young, intelligent-faced wife and small daughter visited him, and Patti quietly noticed the couple's obvious love for each other.

'Well, even if there's no miracle,' she said to herself, 'Mrs Baker is going to stay by him. I suppose it's his work that worries him as much as anything. If he's in public relations . . . So many people can't treat any kind of obvious injury in a normal way.'

Glenn Baker went down to Theatre early the next morning and was back from the recovery ward but still very groggy when Patti came on duty at three. At four, Dr Pritchard came into the ward to check his patient's condition just as Patti was very gently and carefully sliding a loop of the tubing of the intravenous drip away from where it had accidentally fallen across Mr Baker's heavily bandaged face.

'The trolley must have been bumped,' Angus said, taking her by surprise as she had not heard his approach. He had evidently guessed what she was doing, however.

'Yes. Mr Kosek knocked it on his way to the bathroom. Mr Baker still seems pretty sleepy. I don't think he noticed, but I know how important it is for there to be no pressure or disturbance of the area.'

'Right.' Angus gave her a glance of veiled approbation. 'No need to tell you not to touch the dressings in any way unless I give the word? Or is there?'

'No, there are some things I've managed to pick up in nearly three months on this ward,' Patti retorted gently.

Angus did not acknowledge the remark, but turned in silence to bend over Mr Baker's still quiet form. Patti had no reason to linger so she went back to the task she had been occupied with before the new patient's intravenous feeding apparatus had claimed her attention.

Three days later she and Sister Barrett were both occupied in changing the linen of Arthur Donahue in the bed on Glenn Baker's right. Nicola was not in a good mood that day, nor was she working particularly well. Patti knew that she had a bad headache and had lain awake late the night before with severe dysmenorrhoea.

It might have been better to stay in bed, but even if
Nicola Barrett was a little too cold to be likeable, she was
conscientious and had struggled bravely on to the afternoon shift.

'That corner needs straightening, Patti,' she said
shortly, towards the end of the process.

'Does it? Yes, sorry, I see.' Beds still occasionally
caused their old problems.

Sister Barrett's tiredness showed in impatience at that
moment, and she tugged the top sheet before Patti had
gripped it properly herself, with the result that she
stepped back and put out an instinctive hand towards
Glenn Baker's bed to recover her balance. Old Mr
Donahue, on top of whom the bed was being made,
clucked his tongue in irritation, but Patti was looking
across at the next bed.

Nicola had recovered herself quickly enough to avoid
actually falling on to Glenn's delicately dressed and still
very tender face, but her arm brushed it and disturbed
the gauze visibly. The patient groaned and moved a
bandaged hand towards the area.

'Don't touch it, please, Mr Baker,' Nicola said
quickly. 'I'm sorry about the pain. I slipped. I really am
terribly sorry, but no damage has been done. Can I have
a look please?'

She coaxed his hand back to his side and bent over the
disturbed dressing.

'Do you need any help, Sister Barrett?' Patti asked,
uncertain whether to continue with Mr Donahue's bed
alone.

'No, just finish there quickly would you? Mr Donahue
shouldn't be disturbed by this if we can help it. I'll decide
what to do about this dressing.'

Patti finished the bed change with no trouble while

Sister Barrett stood at Mr Baker's side, still looking at the crooked gauze as if lost in thought.

'It has started stinging again,' Glenn Baker said.

He had had a difficult time since surgery. Dr Pritchard's work had been careful and thorough but it was inevitable that the healing process of the delicate facial tissue should be painful, and now the normally easy-going thirty-year-old was exhausted from the strain.

'Can't you do something soon?'

'Yes, we will, Mr Baker,' Nicola Barrett said smoothly, but Patti could see that she was still uncertain. Nicola moved away for a moment and Patti took the opportunity of speaking to her while Glenn could not overhear.

'Could we call Dr Prichard?'

'He's in Theatre,' Sister Barrett replied shortly. 'We'll have to replace the dressing. We can't just put the old one back on. There's a risk that it's contaminated by now.'

'Should we change it though? You know how particular he . . .'

'What else can we do?'

'Sister Barrett!' Kerry, one of the less efficient auxiliaries on the ward hurried up at that moment. 'I need you in the annexe straight away. Sorry, I've mucked something up.'

Patti saw the harassed Sister's face fall into a tired frown.

'That's all I need,' Nicola muttered, but started to follow Kerry.

'Sister Barrett?' Patti said.

'You can change it, Patti. You're easily capable. Just disturb the area as little as you possibly can and I'll explain to Dr Pritchard. He should be here quite soon.'

'Then can't we wait until he comes before we do anything too drastic?'

But Patti's words went unheard as Sister Barrett hurried off in the wake of the anxious Kerry. She took a deep breath and went up to Glenn Baker. The whole affair would probably resolve itself into nothing of importance and would have no unfortunate consequences for the burns victim who had already suffered enough— but nonetheless, it was the most serious professional dilemma Patti had yet faced in her short career.

Dr Pritchard had left explicit instructions that had been confirmed by textbooks Patti had read which stated quite categorically that a nurse must never change the dressing of a patient who has undergone plastic surgery without a specific instruction from the surgeon, and even then such instructions must be carried out punctiliously. Yet Sister Barrett, Patti's senior, had just asked her to violate this rule.

'She's far more senior than me. She must know what she's saying. I'm just being silly to worry,' Patti concluded. 'I'll fix it for you in no time,' she said with a smile to Mr Baker.

'It's all right, it hurts much less now,' he assured her.

Patti prepared the dressing trolley, washed and dried her hands, then took a sterile disposable dressing pack containing the same size and shape of gauze as had originally covered the area. She worked with such concentration and care that she became oblivious to all else, and when she finished the task several minutes later she stood back contentedly, convinced that she had replaced the dressing as exactly as it was possible to do—but all the same, she wished that she, a first-year student, had not been the one to have to do it.

'What have you just done, Nurse Rainer?'

Patti started and her heart thudded as she became aware of Dr Pritchard's tall presence standing next to her. She looked up at him and saw that he had already guessed the answer to his question. He looked coldly angry and she went weak. It was never nice to know that you were about to unleash a storm of anger upon your own head, but when the angry person was Angus Pritchard it was even worse.

'There was a bit of a slip, just a little accident,' she said, trying to keep her voice cool but knowing that the way she seemed to be trying to play down the incident would not gain his respect. 'Sister . . . I had to change part of the dressing.'

'I see.'

He bent towards Mr Baker's face and examined the area with fingers more delicate than even Patti's own much smaller ones had been. She did not know whether he wanted her to stay at his side or not, but did stay, in the absence of any order to the contrary. If the job she had done was as bad as he seemed to expect it was going to be, then he might need her to pass things to him while he redid the dressing. But he straightened not long afterwards and spoke to her.

'I've just had a long day in Theatre,' he said. 'Could you make me some tea?'

'Of course.'

'Thank you. I'll be in the nurses' station in a few minutes. Then I'll take a look at a couple more people after that.'

He turned and walked down the ward to another patient he wanted to check on, while Patti went to the nurses' station to make the tea, thinking that she could use a cup herself. She knew that the calm of his manner would break as soon as they were alone together, and yet she had no defence to prepare. It would be impossible to put the blame on to poor ill Sister Barrett. She would just have to say quietly what she had done and await his reaction.

He came in a minute or two later, just as the electric kettle was beginning to sing.

'Didn't I tell you explicitly that that man's facial dressings were not to be touched?' He launched into the angry words without preamble.

'Yes, you did, but . . .'

'Don't you know how serious the consequences of your action could be? If any kind of infection sets in, all my work could be ruined and that man's face will be worse than it was when I started.'

'Yes, I do know that.'

'Then perhaps you can explain why you ignored the facts—you, a first-year student who is not even qualified to make such a judgment?'

'The dressing was disturbed accidentally and there seemed no alternative but to replace it,' she explained simply.

'How long ago did this happen?'

'A few minutes before you arrived.'

'Then couldn't you have waited before taking any action?'

'Yes, I suppose so. I'm sorry.'

'I'm not sure what I should do about this,' Angus Pritchard said now. The tension of his anger moulded his body into hard, arrogant lines, but even when his blue-green eyes were cold, as now, they still had the power to make Patti melt inside. 'There's nothing to be done, I suppose. I think you've taken my point. But please remember that in future it is not your place to take any initiative in this kind of work.'

'Yes, I understand.'

Angus reached out a cool hand, took the jug of milk to add more to his tea, then drained the cup in a few quick mouthfuls.

'I haven't got time to be relaxing. There are still several patients to see. Where is Sister Barrett? I'll need her.'

'I'm not sure. She was helping Kerry Chapman, one of the auxiliaries, in the ward annexe. Shall I go and find her?'

'Yes please, if you wouldn't mind.' The courtesy of the request was a pure formality.

Patience left the nurses' station quickly and went in search of Sister Barrett. She found Kerry in the annexe but the Sister was no longer with her.

'Where has Nicola gone?' she asked.

'To the bathroom. She's really not well. I told her she ought to go off sick,' Kerry said.

'Is she all right by herself?'

'She says so. She says she'll stay in the bathroom for a while, or sit down in the nurses' station, and go off if she's not feeling better in half an hour.'

'I'll ring to warn the roster staff that we might need a relief sister for the rest of the shift,' Patti said.

'Yes, I think you should. Poor Sister Barrett looked terrible.'

Patti returned to the nurses' station and made the call. Angus was still waiting, standing just outside as he checked through a sheaf of record cards.

'I'm sorry, Dr Pritchard, Sister Barrett is feeling ill. She's in the bathroom and is going to sit down for fifteen minutes, then see if she can continue. Would I be able to help you with the patients you need to see?'

'Yes, of course,' he said shortly. 'It's just routine—taking notes about treatment—careful notes—and having a few pieces of equipment at the ready.'

He began to walk away as he spoke and Patti followed behind feeling nervous. After his recent reprimand she guessed that the surgeon would continue to be especially cool and critical of her work, and trepidation about this was not a helpful addition to the complex emotions she already felt whenever Angus Pritchard was near.

The doctor spent twenty minutes on the ward and to Patience's relief the work she helped him with was routine, just as he had said it would be. It was when he was nearly ready to leave that Sister Barrett finally appeared, looking worse than ever now. She stood leaning heavily against the door of the nurses' station.

'Dr Pritchard, I'm sorry. I'm ready to help now. Or are you finished?'

'I'm finished,' he replied. 'And in any case, you're in no state to continue work. Nurse Rainer, you'll know how to ring the roster staff and arrange for a replacement.'

'I've already warned them that we might be wanting one,' Patti said, glad that for once she could show him some efficiency on her part. 'I'll just confirm it.'

'Sister Barrett, I'll take you down to Reception and we can probably arrange for someone to drive you home. You do live away, don't you?'

'Yes. Thank you . . . I'm sorry to be such a nuisance.'

'Let's not waste any more time,' Angus Pritchard said, speaking coolly. 'Nurse Rainer, you'll have to tell Sister Gibson that there is no qualified sister on the ward until the replacement arrives and then you must continue with your routine work. I won't be coming back after I've taken Sister Barrett down.'

'Yes, Doctor,' Patti murmured, watching him help Sister Barrett into her coat and offer a supportive arm.

Nicola leaned on it gratefully, looking flushed and dazed with fever now. It looked like a bad case of flu and it was to be hoped that Sister Barrett had not infected any of the patients on the ward.

Patti stood watching the pair as they progressed down the corridor. Angus had not said goodbye to her, but it was not to be expected that he would after his recent anger against her. Clipped instructions would be all she would receive from him for some time, probably. His tall lean body was still bending solicitously towards Nicola. Patti had been hoping that the ill sister would explain that the decision to change the dressing had been hers, but it was obvious now that the whole thing had gone completely out of her thoughts. Patti could not blame her for this, of course, but it was unfortunate.

How could she ever hope to win Angus's liking now? Or was it even more than this she had been hoping for?

I'm jealous! Patti realised with horror as the pair disappeared around a corner in the now-quiet corridor, the surgeon's capable arm still supporting the sick nurse. Just because she has the excuse to lean on him, and because he's giving her all his attention! I'd better get put on a medical ward for the next three months, not another surgical one, or this stupid crush will never go away!

CHAPTER SEVEN

IT WAS April and spring had come. The harsh dark lines of the hospital building had been softened once again by foliage, and beds of daffodils gave colour that cheered hearts which were feeling wearied and demoralised after the long winter.

Walking back to the nurses' home after a morning shift on one particularly fine Thursday, Patience felt her spirits lift almost unbearably. She had been sent to a ward that dealt largely with respiratory complaints and had found the increase in patients over the winter months tiring and sometimes distressing. Most of the people she treated were chronic sufferers who would only be given temporary relief by a spell in hospital, and Patti realised that she had a tendency to become too involved in worry and anxiety about many of her patients.

As well as this, it was impossible to say that her painful awareness of Angus Pritchard had been cured by three months spent on a ward in a wing of the hospital that was very far from any of the places to which his work brought him. They had literally not spoken since her last day on Jackson Ward, not because he had ignored her or snubbed her in any way, but simply because their paths had not crossed and he had not sought her out, of course.

Patti wondered if he ever thought of the incident of Glenn Baker's facial dressings. She did, often—playing it over in a dozen different ways that might have had less

114

unpleasant consequences for herself. After that day there had been a tense time during which she was sure that Glenn's scarring would be worse as a result of her action, but finally the bandages had come off and both Dr Pritchard and the patient himself had been extremely pleased.

Patience had tried to avoid Angus as much as possible on the ward, and if he had noticed he hadn't seemed to care. He had never referred again to his anger against her, but she sensed a coolness in him and responded to it in the same vein, so that it soon became a habit between them and was unbroken even by Christmas and New Year festivities on the ward.

Nicola had not returned to Jackson Ward until Patti's last day there. Her influenza had had such severe complications that she had been ordered to convalesce for several weeks before working again. It was very fortunate that only one patient, due to go home a couple of days later, had caught the infection, and in a very mild form.

But even after Patti had been moved to Milsom Ward, she had been too aware of Angus Pritchard, listening guiltily every time she heard his name mentioned around the hospital, although she never ventured to ask anything about him. He had been away for four weeks in February and March, Patti knew, attending an important conference on micro-surgical techniques on the West Coast of America. She had overheard two doctors talking about this—and then, coincidentally, the very next day, she had been leafing through a magazine and had seen the lovely face of Dr Pritchard's dinner companion that night at the Italian restaurant staring out at her.

Marianne Moore headed for stardom, the heading of

the article had read. It seemed that the actress had
achieved a big break after several years of playing
frustrating minor roles, and was now shooting a film . . .
on the West Coast of America.

But the coming of spring had suddenly brought Patti
out of the pointless mood of depression she had dragged
herself into. She would be able to go for a good long ride
this weekend at her parents' place and get some of these
cobwebs out of her system once and for all.

There was a hand-delivered note for her in the R
pigen-hole of the letter-rack in the foyer, along with one
or two other unimportant pieces of mail, but she waited
till she had reached her room and thrown off her cap,
stockings and shoes before reading it.

'*Dear Patience*,' ran the assured black scrawl of Angus
Pritchard, '*Your parents have kindly invited me to stay
for the weekend and suggested that we could travel down
together. This will cut the length of your visit a little, as I
cannot leave until noon on Saturday, and would prefer to
be back on Sunday night. Please ring me to arrange the
details.*'

The phone number of his flat followed, and the note
was signed with his full name.

'As if he thinks there might be more than one Angus in
my life,' Patti thought. 'Or perhaps it's to emphasise the
distance between us—as if I'd ever forget that!'

She had a stupid impulse to hurry to the phone straight
away, but she squashed it and changed into a colourful
candy-striped top and yellow canvas-weave pants as a
celebration of the spring mood, even though it had
ebbed slightly now. Part of her—the silly, schoolgirl
part—looked forward to this unexpected chance to
spend time alone in his company. The sensible side took
control though, and pointed out that the weekend was

far more likely to be awkward, unpleasant and embarrassing. His note was so formal, no wasted words at all, which suggested that he had only accepted her parents' proposal out of politeness.

Defiantly, Patti even sat down in the common room with a cup of coffee and a book for half an hour before trying the number he had given her. Her heart was thudding as she pressed the cold plastic of the receiver to her ear and dialled. It was ridiculous. And she hung on for a long time, listening to the rhythmic burr of the ringing tone, before she decided that he was not going to answer. Probably he had dropped the note off during his lunch break and was not yet home from the hospital.

It was only a quarter to four. None of her friends were about as they all had B shifts that week. She decided to go for a walk to take advantage of a day that was unusually gorgeous for this time of year. Topping her casual outfit with a light, waterproof jacket in an up-to-the-minute white fabric that had almost the texture of paper, and running a comb through bouncing curls that seemed glad to be liberated from their work-a-day knot, she was ready to leave five minutes later.

It was a nature walk—as much as a walk could be, here in the city. Patti chose a route through a well-kept park which emerged into streets of houses and flats that also had pleasant and sizeable gardens. She was deliberately crazy, taking time to smell flowers, swing on a swing, walk balancing along the low log fences that separated different areas of the park and even to hug the rough trunks of a tree or two.

A while later, in a quiet street, after she was hit on the head—fairly painlessly—by a tennis ball being used in a children's game, she returned it with spirit and was made a temporary member of the team.

'Having a good game?' Angus Pritchard had caught up to her unseen.

She laughed and blushed but could think of nothing to say in reply. He would think her absurdly childish.

'I see you got my message,' the surgeon went on.

'Yes, but how did you . . . ?'

'You're on the way to my place. Didn't you know?'

'No . . . I mean, it's just a coincidence. I was going for a walk to . . . to enjoy spring,' she explained, feeling foolish. In dark casual pants, a white shirt and deep rust-coloured jacket he looked very cool and his smile was disconcertingly gorgeous, throwing her pulses into a galloping beat.

'I could see that,' he said now. 'I've been behind you almost all the way, but I only managed to catch up here when you stopped to play ball. And you mean you're not on your way to see me to make arrangements about the weekend?'

'No. I had no idea you lived in this area. I somehow thought it was in the other direction,' she replied, waving a vague hand.

'When in fact this is my block of flats right here.' He indicated a small and tidy building of pale stone. 'Come in for coffee.'

'Oh, I can't,' Patti replied wildly.

'Expected back?'

'No, but . . . What about hospital gossip?'

'I think we're safe by now, don't you?' he said drily. 'It must be weeks since we exchanged so much as a word.'

'Months,' she blurted out, regretting the word instantly. It practically gave away the secret of her feelings for him.

'That long? I haven't been counting. So of course you'll come in?'

'All right.'

He led the way into the building and up one flight of stairs, while Patti began to feel a mounting curiosity about how he lived here. Angus opened the door to reveal a narrow passageway, but beyond that a spacious open-plan flat—one bedroom, a small study and a sitting-room which was separated from the kitchen only by a sweep of clean white worktop.

'Sit down,' he commanded. 'I'll make coffee.'

'I can help.'

'You'd only slow things down. I have the process down to a fine art,' he grinned.

Patience sat on a low, comfortable divan and watched him prepare a rich brew of coffee using the French system of filter-paper and jug.

The flat was lovely. Tranquil, bright, and very taste-fully decorated. He had furnished it himself, she had no doubt of that. The quality of the Berber rugs, the fat brown velvet-upholstered easy chairs and divan, the pictures and prints that broke the expanse of matt cream-painted walls—all bespoke the taste of an intelli-gent individual, rather than an anonymous landlord's cheap and motley arrangement.

Angus did not look at her as he moved about the kitchen, so she felt safe enough to take frequent covert glances at him. He had been pale through the winter, but California had obviously been sunny and there must have been breaks in the conference schedule. For he was lightly tanned now. Patti took in once again his Roman nose, high cheekbones and firm, well-shaped lips, then her eyes strayed to wide shoulders, a slim but strong torso, long legs that beneath the dark trousers would be sculptured with athletic muscles . . .

It's too much, she thought. I shouldn't have come. I

should have arranged the details of the weekend with him out in the street and said I had to get back quickly.

'Milk?' The question cut across her thoughts.

'Yes, please.'

As he had done at the café, he took his black, she noticed. Then he came over and sat beside her on the divan, draping his body casually in its comfortable curves.

'How's life on Milsom Ward?' he asked.

'Good. Although draining. So many chronic cases,' she replied a little awkwardly. 'I'll be moving soon. I'm quite glad, really.'

'Know where you're going yet?' The question was laconic and lazy. He was just making polite conversation, Patti realised sadly.

'No, I find out at the end of next week.'

'Any preferences?'

'Not really.' Patti tried to concentrate exclusively on his questions and her own replies, but it was hard. 'I'm interested in everything, because at this stage it's all new and I'm learning every day. Something quite different from the two I've had so far would be nice. Obstetrics or Paediatrics.'

'What about Theatre?' he asked casually, studying her.

'I'd love to try it,' Patti replied honestly. 'But it's unusual for a first-year nurse to be sent there. I'm keeping my fingers crossed though.'

'A lot of people don't like it,' he said now.

'I know,' Patti replied. 'And of course I don't know that I will till I try it, but I'm fairly certain that I will. It's a place where techniques are advancing very quickly, and I think I'm attracted by the tension and drama of it as well.'

Angus did not reply to this, and Patti wondered whether he thought her reasons sounded silly. There was a small silence before he spoke again, changing the subject.

'You're in a very spring-like mood today.' He flicked a casual eye over her crazy-coloured clothes and she flushed slightly, remembering all the things he must have seen her do if he had, as he said, followed her all the way from the hospital.

'Yes, I love this time of year,' she confessed. 'But you must think I'm a complete child . . .'

'Kissing trees and balancing on railings? I think it's wonderful,' he said. 'And adorable . . .'

There was a pause, during which he looked for too long and too warmly into her eyes. She blushed and looked down, then he continued, breaking the mood.

'I wish more people dared to do such things. And I wish I felt relaxed enough to do them more often myself.'

She laughed, not quite believing him; then there was a silence which to her was filled with unspoken words, before he continued in a more neutral way with a couple of anecdotes about his trip to America. They had both finished their coffee before he spoke about the weekend and the arrangements they had to make.

'You don't mind missing Friday night at your parents'?' he asked.

'No, I go down there often enough,' she said. 'It's very kind of you to offer to drive me down.'

'It's kind of your parents to ask me,' he countered. 'And only sensible for me to drive you down. I'll pick you up at noon then?'

'Yes. If that's the time that suits you best.'

'It is. And we'll have lunch on the way.'

'I'm sure Mother will have something . . .'

'I'll be too hungry to wait,' Angus said with finality, not allowing Patti to protest further.

Another silence fell and Patti decided that he was probably waiting for her to go. He had been incredibly pleasant and friendly today, but she would not risk stretching his charm too far. She stood up, leaving her empty cup on a smoothly-finished wooden coffee table. He rose too, guessing her intentions, and walked with her to the door, not offering her another cup.

'Till Saturday then,' Angus said. They stood in the tiny passage from which the bathroom and bedroom opened.

'Yes, and again, thank you.'

He stretched out a hand to open the door for her, a movement which brought them very close together in the confined and dimly-lit space, and suddenly, before Patti could take in what was happening at all, he had bent towards her and touched her lips in a gentle kiss.

At first she responded as if to the brief kiss of a friend, but then his arms had enclosed her slim frame and he was beginning a slow, deliberate exploration of the soft curve of her mouth. She was instantly aware of his warmth, of the faint, musky scent of his after-shave and of a melting current that coursed through her and left her weak. She closed her eyes, wanting with the rational part of herself to pull away, but too full of the unimagined delight of being in his arms. She could stay forever like this . . .

The telephone rang with a loud, jangling note that bruised her ears and broke the mood instantly. She felt Angus stiffen, hesitate, then release her.

'Damn!'

The word was muttered very low as he strode into the

sitting-room. Patti stood for a few seconds, leaning a hot cheek against the half-open door and feeling her heart thudding. Would she stay? Wouldn't he want to speak to her, say something which would explain what that kiss had meant to him?

'Hallo?' Angus had picked up the phone and the word was spoken with suppressed impatience; then his tone suddenly changed. 'Marianne You're in London? I didn't expect you till next week! Shooting finished ahead of schedule . . . ?'

Soundlessly, Patti let herself out of the flat and walked quickly down the stairs.

CHAPTER EIGHT

THE MEMORY of Angus's kiss stabbed at Patti again and again over the next day. She thought about ringing her parents up and cancelling the weekend. She could ask them to ring and tell Angus. Or she could say she was sick. Of course he wouldn't believe it, but that didn't matter.

Then she realised that he would probably make an apologetic phone call to her parents too, and that would sound odd. Perhaps it would be better to leave the cancellation to him and to do nothing herself. There would be a phone call this evening from her father to say that he would be picking her up after all; Angus had come down with flu, had had to work unexpectedly, or even the truth.

After all, why not? His girlfriend had returned from America sooner than expected after the shooting of her film, and Angus wanted to spend some time with her. Very natural, and very understandable.

By half-past ten on Friday evening, when Patti realised that her father's call was not going to come, it was too late to do anything about it herself. A feeling of anger had begun to replace her initial response of warmth mingled with confusion and pain.

Dr Pritchard's girlfriend had been safely on the other side of the Atlantic, or so he had thought, and in the meantime a casual encounter of some kind—because who knew how far he had been planning for it to lead?—with a willing young nurse would help to pass the lonely hours.

But when the lovely actress turned out to be in town after all, it seemed that the nurse's very existence was forgotten. As Patti was walking away from Angus's flat as quickly as she could, she had half-expected to hear running footsteps behind her and his voice calling her name, calling her back to say . . . What? That Marianne meant nothing to him, and the kiss they had just shared had made him realise that she, Patti, was the one he cared about?

Lying restless and miserable in bed on Friday night, Patti almost laughed aloud to think that it was only a little more than twenty-four hours ago she had sketched out the naive scenario. She had turned into the hospital grounds before she finally made herself believe that he was not coming, and was no doubt still on the phone exchanging news and loving words with Marianne.

But it did seem at least that he was not going to back out of the agreed weekend at her parents' place. Patti had to respect him a little bit for that. As Saturday morning passed slowly by, however, her dread of meeting him again—and alone!—grew greater and greater.

She wanted to hate him, and did, but keeping up the feeling in the face of the onslaught of his body on her senses would not be easy. She had succumbed so easily and shamelessly to that kiss, surprising herself by the strength of her response and no doubt surprising him even more. Just how far would he have succeeded in taking her, and how far would she have willingly gone, if the phone had not rung when it did?

This morning would be different, Patti determined. There would be no chink in her defences. Angus Pritchard would not see the expression of worry and uncertainty that both Lisa and Janice had commented on yesterday at dinner.

It was now eleven. Her overnight bag was packed and she was already dressed in comfortable travelling clothes—navy blue stretch jeans and an angora pullover of deep water-melon pink. There was time for a solid hour of work on her latest nursing assignment, which would drive away any thoughts of Dr Angus Pritchard.

She was waiting for him in the foyer at twelve as promised, and he was just four minutes late—a margin sufficiently small to mean that he could get away without an apology, but which she felt was a deliberate slight, nonetheless. There had been a few moments in which she had been indecisive about her choice of clothing, tempted to choose an outfit that was defiantly dressy and sophisticated. Now she was glad she had not. There was going to be no transparent indication of her feelings.

'That's all the luggage you've brought?' Angus said cheerfully. 'Just put it in the back seat.'

Patti replied adequately, politely, and very coolly. Then for almost half an hour they drove largely in silence. Angus offered the occasional comment about the things they passed *en route*, but Patti initiated only one piece of conversation.

'You should turn off here. I mean . . . unless you know of a short-cut to Wellham.'

'We're having lunch, remember?'

'There are a few places further along . . .'

'It's a glorious day and I know of a perfect pub-restaurant where we can sit outside. It's not far.'

Obviously he was going to ignore her attempt to get this tension-filled journey over and done with as quickly as possible. They turned almost immediately down a leafy avenue and a few minutes later swung into the gravelled forecourt of a pub that was old and rustic without making too much of a show of the fact.

Angus led the way confidently through a low interior to a courtyard at the back where trees and shrubs newly in leaf and bud did not prevent warm sunshine from falling on to tables prettily laid out with red and white check cloths. Menus were brought and Patti scanned hers briefly, then obstinately insisted on ordering the simplest thing possible, a ploughman's lunch, even though Angus made it clear that he would have preferred her to join him in a more elaborate meal.

Tension increased noticeably as Patti picked her way through the admittedly delicious bread, cheese, chutney and salad, while Angus consumed turkey breast and mushroom pâté in a feather-light pastry crust. He spoke at last, just as Patti finished her plate.

'Can't we talk about the other day, Patience? Something is obviously . . .'

'There's nothing to say,' she cut in, ignoring the beguiling warmth of his tone as soon as she could find words. 'It's a moment in the past, that's all. Something to be forgotten.'

'And not referred to again?' His query was cool and clipped.

'Exactly. That's best, don't you think? In the circumstances . . .'

'Quite.'

Silence fell again, but Patti was not bored. She was far too occupied in trying to forget how unutterably attractive she still found the man who sat opposite her and how much she would have liked to have been able to reply in a very different tone to the words he had just spoken.

They arrived at her parents' place at a little after two, and the presence of Mr and Mrs Rainer and Patti's three younger brothers dissipated the strain in her relationship with Angus considerably—for the time being, at least.

Patti was soon spirited off to the far corner of the garden to see her brothers' new tree-house, and gratified them exceedingly by her willingness to climb up into it, survey the view from the 'crow's nest', swing dangerously from a lovely bendy branch, and drink the rather smoky tea brewed by Timothy in an old kettle on the fireplace of stones that the boys had constructed on the ground below. Angus was safely ensconced in the study with her father, discussing goodness knew what—and anyway, it did not matter now if he did think that she was utterly childish.

At four they all met up for tea, then it was Angus's turn for a tour of the outdoors, while Patti sat in the kitchen with her mother, catching up on news, and then paid a long overdue visit to her horse Becky, who was stabled and cared for by a keen horsewoman in the village.

It was only when everyone gathered for a family supper later that evening that Patti was forced into an awareness of Angus again.

'So you're still in that flat near the hospital, Angus?' Mr Rainer said.

'Yes,' Angus replied. 'I like it. It's quiet and big enough, with the study, and close to the hospital. I could afford to buy something, but I'm not sure quite what, or where, at this stage.'

'Of course,' Mrs Rainer agreed. 'You may marry, and that could change all your plans and priorities. May I be terribly inquisitive and ask if there is anything like that in the wind? You're much too eligible a bachelor to stay that way for much longer.'

Patti stared down at the honey-oozing crumpet on her plate, steeling herself to hear a smooth acknowledgement that Angus's engagement to Marianne Moore would shortly be announced.

'Actually, I'm going to disappoint you there,' he smiled. 'There's no one serious in my life, though I hope there soon will be. I have women friends, of course—one or two very good ones. But it's not always as easy for surgeons to find the right person as some people suppose.'

Mrs Rainer laughed, evidently taking his explanation as a light fob-off of her curiosity. Patience did not know what to think. Probably her mother's reaction was the right one. Or had there been an undertone of more serious intent? Her carefully built-up coldness and determined dislike crumbled. The words *could* have been meant for her, couldn't they?

Angus might have been trying to say that Marianne Moore was and always had been just a friend, and Thursday's overpowering kiss had meant something to him after all.

No, she was being a naive little idiot even to consider the possibility. She had been influenced by too many lightweight happy endings in films. It was far more likely that Angus simply did not want to reveal Marianne's importance in his life until they had come to a definite arrangement about their future together. And after Patti's own assertion today at lunch that she wanted to put their kiss behind her forever, Angus hadn't even considered that his words might be able to be interpreted in two ways.

The subject of conversation had changed now.

'What about tomorrow, Angus? Patti will want to ride if there's even an attempt at fine weather. What about you? Margaret Kendall, who keeps Patti's horse, hires out a few good animals.'

'I'd love to ride,' he said. 'If Patience doesn't mind?'

He looked at her, and the look was not simply a casual glance. She knew he was asking for some kind of permission—more than just permission to accompany her on her ride. What would she be telling him if she said yes? That she had forgiven his kiss and its consequences? She did not yet know if she had, or what her forgiveness would mean to him. But in any case, in front of her parents it would be impossible to say that he could not come with her.

'Of course not, Dr Pritchard. It would be nice to have a companion.'

'*Dr Pritchard?*' Mrs Rainer queried with a laugh. 'Surely you don't have to call him that away from the hospital?'

'I think I should,' Patti said before Angus could speak. She was embarrassed. 'I mean, I don't know. Everything is very formal there. I'm so lowly compared with him . . . I couldn't possibly call him Angus on the ward, and I'd be afraid I'd do so by accident if I started doing it here.'

'Poor thing!' Mrs Rainer said, laughing again. 'I had no idea hospitals were so tediously formal. Don't they know by now that you are friends outside of your work?'

'We're not,' Patti blurted out, increasingly aware of Angus's silence. 'I've tried to play it down. Your asking Dr Pritchard to introduce me to Sister Clayton and Sister Taylor brought me nothing but trouble. Sorry, Mother . . . and Dr Pritchard . . . but it's true. It doesn't matter now, though, so let's drop the subject, shall we?'

Patti got up and began clearing away the supper

things, biting her lip and wishing she had not spoken so hastily. Angus followed her into the kitchen with a pile of plates and they washed up together as Mrs Rainer cleared and stacked the remaining things.

'I owe you an apology,' the surgeon said quietly to Patience as he wiped the cutlery after Mrs Rainer had finished her part of the task and left them to it.

'You do?'

'Yes. I don't mean to be rude about your mother—she was simply concerned about your welfare—but I was very reluctant about introducing you to Sister Clayton and Angela Taylor, and I thought it was your idea. I thought that you wanted to use me to gain some instant status at the hospital, and I judged you quite harshly for it. I'm sorry.'

'It doesn't matter, it's in the past,' Patti said for the second time that day, but truthfully this time.

'You must be starting to have a very full past,' Angus said, obviously thinking of what she had said at lunch, too.

'Not really,' Patti replied lightly.

The next day dawned fine. Patti, rustling to the bathroom in a silky blue nightdress, passed the open door of the spare room and saw that Angus was awake. He lazed in rumpled bed-clothes that matched the deliciously untidy state of his chestnut hair, and was reading an American current affairs magazine as he sipped a cup of tea which Mrs Rainer must have brought him.

He glimpsed Patti on her way past and stopped her with a few words.

'I'm looking forward to the ride. It's going to be a glorious day.'

'Yes, it is,' Patti agreed, embarrassed at having been caught so inadequately dressed. Her hair was a bush too, and her face still creased and stiff with sleep. She started to walk on but he spoke again.

'If it was summer, or if this was somewhere down on the Mediterranean, you could ride dressed like that, side-saddle. You'd look like a medieval maiden in a fairytale.'

'Hardly!'

She escaped this time, disturbed by his words and by the long frank look that had accompanied them—not to mention the effect on her senses of his figure in the wide bed. He had been sitting up, propped against pillows, and whatever he might have been wearing on his lower half, he certainly had nothing on the upper, revealing a fact which Patience had long suspected—that his chest was a perfect sculpture of tanned muscles and regularly-patterned dark hair.

After a solid breakfast of eggs, bacon and tomato, as well as toast and coffee, they were ready to set out. Patti carried a small leather saddle-bag containing a light packed lunch, as they had decided to go quite a distance and eat picnic-style, planning to return at about four. Angus carried a thermos of hot water for tea and wet-weather jackets in case the day did not fulfil its promise of sunshine.

They had a marvellous time. It was so warm that Patti wore short sleeves for an hour, taking off her peacock blue cotton pullover to reveal a bright pink V-necked T-shirt. Angus was in denim jeans and a matching shirt that hugged his lean figure closely and distracted Patti terribly with the way it revealed every economical move-ment he made on the big chestnut, Cleland, that Mrs Kendall had chosen for him at her stables.

Patti's own darker Becky behaved impeccably, and Patti experienced an exhilaration she had not known for

a long time as every sense was crammed with impressions—the heat of the sun on her back, an occasional puff
of wind raking through her loose hair, the refreshing
chill of patches of shade.

By lunch-time both of them were hungry and enjoyed
nearly an hour of lazy eating and conversation among
the fragrant grasses of a sunny field, with the cold gurgle
of a stream as background while the two horses grazed
and dozed.

Angus and Patti got to know each other that day,
exchanging opinions, experiences, stories and jokes.
But there were long periods of companionable silence
too, in which they revelled in the sounds of spring—
birds, the rustling of new leaves, the animal sounds of
the horses and the thud of their hooves playing on
different surfaces in different rhythms.

Most of all, inevitably, it was simply Angus that Patti
enjoyed, for once without bothering herself with nagging uncertainties about how he was feeling in return.
The supper-time conversation of yesterday seemed to
have cleared something in the air between them, and
even if it was nothing more than an honest, cousinly kind
of friendship that he felt for her, even if that kiss had
been just a moment of regretted madness and Marianne
was the important woman in his life, Patti decided that
she would enjoy this day for what it was.

Angus seemed as relaxed and happy as Patti was,
turning to smile at her often, and bursting with a physical
energy that vented itself in long smooth canters and the
occasional gallop that Becky matched gamely under
Patti's guidance.

'You ride so well,' Patti said frankly as they walked
home from Mrs Kendall's at nearly five o'clock—later
than planned.

'So do you,' Angus returned. 'And yet you stuck at being a stable-hand for so long.'

'Two years,' Patti nodded.

'Why didn't you go in for show-jumping?'

'I don't have the temperament,' she replied without regret. 'That single-minded need to win. I love riding, and I always will, but other things are important too.'

'Such as?' He asked the question meaningfully, as if seeking further insights into her personality, but she tried to reply lightly.

'Now, my work at the hospital. It's giving me a fulfilment that I've known for a long time I would have to find somewhere. There are other outdoorsy things I'd like to try, too. Some of them are rather wild.' With a laugh she listed the ambitions she had spoken of to Lisa. He responded with a surprised but approving lift of his eyebrows and another question.

'Any place in all that for a family of your own?'

'Yes. One day.'

Just then they arrived at the house.

It was after six by the time the two were ready to leave to return to Ricky's. Both had showered and dressed in fresh clean clothes before having a long cool drink and a last chat with Patti's parents. Mrs Rainer suggested that they stay on for a light Sunday evening meal, but Angus said that he would prefer to get back and Patti was secretly glad, fearing that the good mood of the day could not possibly last too much longer. She would grab a meal at a nearby take-away back in the city.

After Patti had gone upstairs to say a quick goodbye to the boys, who were reluctantly tackling neglected home-work, the two were on their way.

The silence that fell between them for the first half of the journey seemed very different, Patti thought, to the silence that had existed the other two times they had made the trip between Ricky's and Wellham together. This one was relaxed, warm, the silence of two people who are, or could be, familiar with each other's thoughts. It was not until they first began to drive through more populated streets that Angus spoke.

'Tired?'

'A bit, but in a nice way. The shower and the clean clothes did me good.'

'The dress certainly does you good.' He glanced quickly across at her lithe form, clad now in a dress of burgundy patterned in tiny flowers and topped by a light velveteen jacket of rich black. The chunky gold necklace that nestled around a creamy throat revealed by the sweetheart neckline gave colour and accented the white-gold highlights of her hair. 'It seems a pity to waste it.'

'Sorry?'

'Would you like to eat somewhere with me? I didn't want to put your parents out, and I wanted to get the drive over with, but we have to dine sometime.'

'You'd rather eat alone.'

'I wouldn't.'

'All right then. Something fairly quick.' Part of her thought that on the contrary it would be nice to spend a very long, very slow evening with him at a restaurant— but of course, no hint of this feeling could be revealed.

'If you want it that way. Do you have anything in mind?'

'Not really. I still don't know this area terribly well.'

'My choice then?'

'Yes please.'

They stopped a while later at a small but good quality Tandoori house where the surgeon was evidently known, judging by the waiter's greeting and subsequent attentiveness. They dispensed with aperitifs but each chose a light entree of vegetable-filled pastries accompanied by a deliciously piquant sauce. After this, Angus chose a hot Madras chicken dish while Patti had a fragrant plate of spiced lamb and spinach in yoghurt.

And again they talked, easily and comfortably, about a dozen different things while a bottle of crispy chilled white wine slipped down almost without Patience noticing. After the long, tiring day outdoors, the sun, the drive, and now this meal, she felt very light-headed as they left the restaurant, found the car, and drove the mile or so back to the hospital.

'I'll walk you upstairs,' Angus said as he pulled into a short-stay parking place at the side of the building.

'There's no need.'

He took no notice of this, though, and they went through the foyer together. Patti thought of how he had walked through this same place nearly eight months ago, an expression of scarcely concealed impatience and dislike set in his features. Things seemed so different now. He wasn't arrogant at all. As Lisa had said, the distance and coolness he sometimes affected was simply one of the requirements of his position. Today he had been so warm. Could something be going to happen between them?

Patti, feeling that she was viewing the matter dispassionately, thought that it might—and thought that she probably wanted it to.

The foyer was deserted. She looked at the electric clock on the wall and saw that it was past ten already. They had taken longer over the meal than she would have thought. Again she remembered the last time

Angus had been here with her and how then there had been curious girls staring at them from the group of chairs they were just passing.

Idly, Patti looked across and saw the little table where magazines were kept for anyone waiting for a nurse to come down. Then suddenly, shattering her serene mood, a familiar face stared at her from the cover of a new women's magazine.

Marianne Moore! And the caption, in large bold yellow letters below the photo read: *New Star Returns to England—and Love*.

Angus did not hear the little cry that escaped Patti's lips. He was already at the lift, pressing the call button. She joined him, staring down and praying that he would not guess, or had not guessed already from her behaviour today, the foolish fantasies she had been weaving about him.

Everything appeared in a new light again now, because she did not doubt that the love referred to by the magazine was love for the man who stood at her side. Patti and Angus had spent a wonderful weekend together, but no doubt Angus had seen it as a family obligation and had probably explained it to Marianne as such. Driving the daughter of his godfather down to her home, riding with her, driving back and having a meal with her.

Oh, he did like her as a friend. In spite of the awkward moments they had had in the past there was no doubt of that, and perhaps even his kiss had been something he thought she would take as a light piece of flattery . . .

They had reached the darkened end of her corridor while these unhappy realisations burned in Patti's mind, and Angus did not seem to have noticed that there was anything wrong. Patti steeled herself for their goodbyes, fumbling for her key in the leather bag she carried. She found it finally and turned her face to him.

'Thank you for the weekend,' she said. 'For the drive, and riding together, and the meal.'

'Thank *you*, Patti,' he said. 'For your parents' hospitality . . . and just for you.'

'Good night, then.'

'Patti . . .'

Before she could move, turn her head aside, say no or do any of the things she knew she should do, she was in his arms and his lips were on hers, warm, urgent, and whispering soft words she could not understand. For a few moments, in spite of everything, she responded, her hand straying to comb through the soft, thick curls at the nape of his neck and her body fitting itself closely to his as he bent to her. No one was about; it was safe—and she didn't care anyway. This moment was the crowning of their glorious day together . . .

But then the thought of Marianne forced itself insistently into the front of her mind. If Patti respected herself, and Marianne, and even Angus, she had to end this now.

'No,' she said, too softly against the firmness of his lips, then more deliberately. 'You don't mean this, and I don't need it. It can't happen. I don't want it.'

For a long time his eyes looked into hers, searching and intensely blue, even in the dim light. Pattie willed herself to appear cold and detached, as if this moment was nothing to her—the fulfilment of a fleeting need perhaps, but certainly nothing special. She would not suffer the humiliation of knowing what he would tell Marianne if he suspected her real feelings . . . 'There's a nurse at the hospital who has rather a crush on me, poor thing . . .' At last his questioning gaze unlocked from her own wooden one.

'All right. I understand. You needn't worry, it won't happen again.'

Then he turned abruptly and was gone in a moment, taking the nearby stairs rather than the lift, his footsteps making rhythmic ringing echoes up and down the bare stairwell.

CHAPTER NINE

'I LOVE HIM,' she said aloud but very softly in her room. 'I'm in love with him.'

What was the point of voicing it? She had known it for ages anyway, without having to say the words. There was no moment that could be pin-pointed as the time when a girlish infatuation and a half-unwilling physical awareness had begun to change into something more real and solid. Even now, she supposed, the feeling would die eventually. It had to. There was nowhere else for it to go, no hope of fulfilment or confession.

If Marianne, with her perfect features and figure, her gorgeous sweep of hair, and her successful and glamorous career, was willing to declare her love publicly on the cover of a magazine, then she must be on the point of marriage or an engagement with the rising young surgeon.

Wouldn't it be an odd match, Patti asked herself, with their two careers pulling in such different directions? But no, it could be seen as a perfect balance. Marianne's world would give Angus an outlet in sophisticated forms of relaxation, and the steady demands of his work and lifestyle would provide an anchor for Marianne. Yes, what could be better?

With this realisation, Patti moved her weary limbs from the stiff attitude in which they had been frozen aimlessly in the centre of her lonely room. There was work tomorrow—an afternoon shift, but she needed to get some shopping done in the morning. Today stretched out behind her, an unbelievably long series of different moods and memories. It was time to end it now in sleep, if she could.

But sleep refused to come for a long time. If only she had seen that magazine on Thursday then none of the events of the past four days need have happened. She would not have gone into Angus's flat for coffee and that first confusing kiss would never have taken place. She could have begun the painful task of squashing her feelings for him out of existence before they had had a chance to become so much stronger. They had learnt so much about each other this weekend, and had understood so much so easily. It was difficult to believe that this did not mean something and that Angus would have preferred to have Marianne's company in the activities he and Patti had shared.

What was Angus doing now? Was he with Marianne or was he alone? Did he have any idea of the havoc he had wrought within her? Surely he must. Wouldn't the wild oscillation in her behaviour towards him tell him that? One minute cold, the next assuming a companionship closer than she had with anyone, and finally those two feverish responses to his kiss.

Patti knew she ought to despise Angus for playing a double game with Marianne and herself—but then, she reflected wearily, perhaps it was just part of the morality of the times. A kiss or two was nothing between sophisticated people. Angus probably assumed that she knew all about Marianne and wasn't trying to deceive her at all. The idea that anyone could fall in love with him on such slight provocation would seem ridiculous to him . . .

After the circular progression of her thoughts had become utterly wearisome, Patti eventually drifted into a deep, tired sleep.

The next morning she got up at eight, determined to look forward to the good things that were happening, not back to Angus's kiss and the awakening of her feelings for him. Next week there would be the challenge of a new ward. Then on Saturday there was to be a party in celebration of both her own birthday and Lisa's, which fell within a month of each other.

The party had been Janice's idea and was timed to fall a week before Lisa's birthday and just under three weeks after Patti's. Patti had just turned twenty-one. She couldn't bury her heart yet . . .

On the way back through the foyer to her room after breakfast, Patti looked across at the magazine table again, thinking that she might as well torture herself by reading the entire article about Marianne Moore and her successes in career and romance, but the magazine was no longer there. This often happened. A girl would 'borrow' it, taking it up to her room to read. Sometimes the magazine would later be returned, but sometimes, regrettably, it would not. In this case it was probably for the best, Patti decided. Wouldn't reading the article only increase her depression?

But later, while out shopping, she couldn't resist the temptation to call in at a newsagent's in search of the magazine. She expected to see the headline and Marianne's face leap out at her from the top of a glossy stack, but the magazine did not seem to be in the shop at all. It could have been one of a dozen, and she had not taken note of the title last night, so could not ask for it by name. It must have been last week's issue, and had already disappeared from the shelves.

Of course, it would be possible to ask around the nurses' home to find out who had taken it, but Patti was not prepared to betray her interest in Angus Pritchard so transparently. She would simply have to forget about the whole thing.

The week passed in a mixture of moods. There were some happy moments on the ward as several of the chronically ill patients were able to return to their own homes now that the warmer weather was beginning. Their ailments had not been cured by their time on the respiratory ward, but many of the symptoms had been relieved for a few months at least.

Patti tried to immerse herself in social activity, resisting a strong temptation to spend unproductive hours in her room brooding. Her circle of friends at the hospital was growing all the time. After all, she had been here for eight months now. It was difficult to believe sometimes. Lisa and Janice were still the most important, but she saw quite a bit of Celine, the French dietician, Rosemary Watson from Jackson Ward, and several others. Mark Stewart visited the recreation lounge on the sixth floor quite often, too. Patience definitely liked him, but not in a romantic way. No, unfortunately there was no hope that *he* would be the one to make her forget her pointless feelings for Angus Pritchard!

In fact it was beginning to look as though Lisa's light-hearted prediction of six months ago would turn out to be right. Mark and Janice were clearly growing interested in each other and Lisa still had her faithful John. Was it just luck that allowed some people to find this kind of happiness apparently without effort?

'No, it's my own fault,' Patti decided. 'Picking on a man like Angus Pritchard to fall for when I've known all along that he was hopelessly out of my reach was asking for trouble.'

On Wednesday, after the student nurses' usual day in

the training building, Sister Taylor unexpectedly asked
Patti to stay behind.

'Come into my office and we'll have a talk,' she said,
smiling to show Patti that it wasn't a reprimand she was
about to receive.

Patti followed the solidly built, cheerful and slightly
fluttery woman into a quiet room that looked out over a
small patch of garden behind the training building. Sister
Taylor explained the reason for the interview without
preamble.

'We've decided to send you to Theatre next week,' she
said. 'It's a little unusual for a first-year student, but we
do it sometimes, so don't feel that you have been singled
out too dramatically. One other girl is being sent there as
well. Felicity Green, who is in Obstetrics at the moment.'

Patti had nodded to all this, not knowing quite how to
reply. Ought she to thank Training Sister? Or take the
news matter-of-factly? Or were there intelligent questions she ought to be asking? Sister Taylor seemed to
have noticed her hesitation.

'You've been interested in that area all along, haven't
you? Or am I wrong? Has this come as a horrible shock?'

'No, no, not at all. I'm very pleased,' Patti hastened to
say. 'I was hoping I would be sent to Theatre, but I didn't
really think I had a chance until next year.'

'It was Angus Pritchard, actually, who put in a word
for you,' Sister Taylor said, growing slightly pink.
'Apparently you've talked about it together. He said you
would like to try Theatre and that from what he had seen
and heard of your work he thought you would do a good
job.'

'Oh . . . You must thank him, then. Or should I?'
Patti stumbled over the words.

Sister Taylor's information had sent her head spinning. Angus had recommended her! It almost amounted to using his influence for her. Was she pleased? Yes. It meant nothing, of course . . . But no, it did mean something, even though it was not what her heart craved. It meant that whatever else he thought of her, or however little she was in his mind, he had noticed her as a nurse and had stored in his memory the comments that other people had made about her work. And what about the facial dressing she had changed against his orders? Had he forgiven that? Or forgotten it?

It seemed now that at least she had earned a certain respect from Angus, even though she could never have his love . . .

Patti collected her thoughts and saw that Sister Taylor was watching her quite closely.

'You're pleased that Angus was the one to recommend you?'

'Um, yes, I suppose so.'

'His girlfriend is a very beautiful woman—and becoming very well-known, too. Have you met her?'

'No. I have seen her, though.' Patti wondered whether Sister Taylor had read the latest news of the lovely actress in the magazine which she herself was so anxious to get hold of.

There was a small pause, then Sister Taylor spoke briskly once more.

'I'd better let you go. Here is your duty roster for the next two weeks. I've noted down where you are to be and when on your first day, as well as a few other details. But have a look over the information later and come and see me if something is not clear.'

Patti rose, responding to the Sister's change of mood. As she left the office, her thoughts were still on their

discussion of Angus Pritchard. It was funny how percep-
tive you became about some things when you were in
love. Perhaps it was natural. Her thoughts revolved so
much around Angus now. Everything he said and did
and everything that was said about him was so important
to her. It had been quite without effort that she had
noticed the slight change in Sister Taylor's manner when
she spoke of the surgeon.

'She's like me,' Patti realised. 'She thinks of him too
much. And she's guessed that I do too.' What a hopeless
situation for both of them!

Janice had received permission to hold the party for
Patience and Lisa in the main ground floor common
room of the nurses' home, and it had now grown into
quite an ambitious project with many girls helping to
decorate the space and an open invitation having been
issued, spread by word of mouth, to a huge number of
people.

Patti was a little embarrassed about the event, hoping
that it would not get out of hand and secretly wishing
that Janice had kept it to the smaller gathering originally
envisaged.

'How will you provide food and drink for everyone?'
she asked her plump friend on Friday night at tea.

'We'll be working on it all day tomorrow while you're
on your last shift in Milsom Ward,' Janice replied. 'You
see, people have taken it as a sort of ward-change
celebration party, and some think it's close enough to
May the first to be a May Day party—there's a second-
year girl from Padstow in Cornwall, where they have
that May Day hobby-horse, so she's very keen about
that . . . Everyone's going to bring food and drink, so it
should be a huge success.'

'Huge being the operative word,' Lisa put in, having sat down with her tray half-way through Janice's speech.

'Are you worried too?' Patti asked her.

'No, like you I'll be at work, so I won't have to help.' Lisa joked.

'I didn't mean that. I meant, might it not get out of hand?' Patti explained.

'I doubt it. Almost everyone will be from the hospital, and we're all pretty responsible, don't you think? There's going to be someone on duty, and I doubt that anyone would gate-crash a party in a nurses' home, so I'm not worried—and I'm prepared to spend Sunday cleaning up.'

Patti frowned. Was she being a complete spoil-sport to be looking forward to this party more with dread than with anticipation? It had been such an effort this week to keep to her resolve of looking cheerfully to the future and to resist the temptation to shut herself away in pointless brooding about the tall, chestnut-haired surgeon . . .

'You have been gloomy this week, Patience Rainer!' Janice said brightly now, echoing Patti's own fears. 'Particularly when fifty per cent of the trouble I'm going to with this party is for you!'

'I know, I'm sorry. I don't know what's the matter with me,' Patti tried to reply with more liveliness, but failed.

'Aren't you well?' Lisa looked genuinely concerned and Janice's face was serious now, too.

'Yes, I'm well. Don't worry about me. I'm just a bit depressed. It'll pass.'

'It's the weather,' Janice said. 'After convincing us that spring was really here, then going back to winter yesterday . . .'

'It's Milsom Ward. We're all different, and your temperament just isn't quite right for a ward with so many chronic patients. You'll be much better in Theatre,' Lisa said, more perceptively but still not guessing the truth—thank goodness!

Patti seized on her suggestion and summoned up some optimism.

'You're probably right. The party will do me good, and I am excited about going into Theatre.'

After this, to Patti's relief, the topic of conversation shifted to nursing, with each of them talking about what they hoped and feared from their next ward. Patti contributed her share, managing to ignore the fact that what *she* most feared about her new duties was working with Angus Pritchard.

Pearly grey clouds lay all over London the next day, but it was mild and Patti enjoyed her last shift on Milsom Ward more than she had expected to. It was heart-warming that the patients seemed sincerely sorry to see her go, having clubbed together to buy her a box of cream-centred chocolates.

At three, after changing out of her uniform into her casual pink cord pants and angora pullover, Patti went straight to the common room to offer her help in setting up the party decorations, but Janice pushed her firmly out of the door again.

'Lisa has already dropped in and I told her this too. We want you to rest. You've been working all day, and as guests of honour you have got to be the most sparkling people here.'

Patti did not try to argue. She was tired. She had not been sleeping terribly well this week, perhaps under-standably, and she owed Janice the courtesy of being lively tonight. After resting for an hour and spending the remainder of the afternoon reading and writing letters, Patti joined her friends for tea in the dining-room and found that everyone was already in a mood of anticipation that she could not help becoming part of. It would be fun to let her hair down later on, dress up in the new outfit she had chosen as a birthday present from her parents, dance to rhythmic music, and have some crazy party conversations.

Later on, when she dressed, she experimented with a more sophisticated style of make-up, nothing too heavy for her age, but nonetheless with bolder lines than she usually used. Mrs Rainer had convinced her that she needed something quite dressy and formal now that she had the chance to become part of a social world that could be more sophisticated than anything she had been used to, and after a couple of hours in two or three London stores, Patti had emerged with a full-skirted dress of stiff flounced taffeta in shimmering sea-tones that changed in different lights.

Tonight, filmy stockings, matching satin-weave slippers and a choker necklace of deep jade stones completed the outfit, and at eight o'clock the only thing Patti had not yet decided on was her hair. Should it be loose and fluffy, or up in one of the high knots into which she could now twist it so expertly?

A knock at the door decided the question. Lisa stood there, sparkling and merry in a low-waisted Twenties-style dress of golden yellow that suited her square-cut straight dark hair very well.

'You look fabulous, Patti!' she exclaimed sincerely. 'The dress is new, isn't it?'

'Yes. A birthday present.'

'That's right. I think you told me. You were going to put it on for me to see but we never got round to it. I love the style, and the colour is perfect. But what about your hair? Are you just wearing it like that?'

'That's what I haven't decided yet . . .'

'I'll do it for you. Will you let me?'

'Of course. But how? I'd like to try something new, but I can't think what.'

'Leave it to me,' Lisa said, with businesslike confidence. 'Sit down and shut your eyes, and don't look until it's finished.'

Lisa's neat, capable fingers were soon at work and ten minutes later Patience was allowed to survey the result. Her hair was piled up in a loose swathe on top of her head and fine tendrils escaped here and there to soften the effect. Lisa was rightly pleased with her work as she stood back and examined it critically.

'I've been practising for ages, and that's the best I've ever done. What do you think?'

'It's lovely. I never could have done it myself.'

'You'll wow every doctor in the room,' Lisa said.

'I'm not interested in wowing doctors,' Patti replied lightly.

She was thinking of Dr Pritchard, but was not worried that he would be at the party tonight. Who would have thought to ask him? He was not part of the general hospital social scene, pursuing his relaxation in other areas. No, if he was not working, Angus Pritchard would be with Marianne Moore tonight, that was certain.

Lisa had not queried Patti's short reply and was now standing by the door, obviously waiting to go downstairs. Probably her faithful John would be waiting in the foyer to join her.

He was, and the three made their way to the streamer-bedecked common room where quite a crowd had already gathered. Patti felt a momentary plunging in her stomach, wondering if, after all, this was really the kind of evening she felt in the mood for, but then the party atmosphere picked her up and swept her along on a tide of frivolous talk—difficult above the noise of music— lively dancing and enjoyable nibbles and drinks.

The time passed in a whirl and the room became increasingly crowded. Several nurses complimented Patti on her dress, and other people whom she had only spoken to briefly around the hospital seemed interested in talking to her. With glowing cheeks and a throat cooled from glasses of fizzy, fruity punch, Patti decided that she was having a very good time and that perhaps the world was not quite such a hopeless place after all.

It was at about ten o'clock that a slight lull in music and dancing occurred, and Patti looked up towards the main door to see a new group of people standing there about to enter. She recognised a couple of young house-men and a surgeon whom she knew, by reputation only, as among the most dashing and eligible figures on the hospital social scene.

There was a taller figure behind them, and when the group began to disperse among the throng, Patti caught sight of Angus Pritchard.

So he had come! It was unexpected and disturbing, but she ignored the hollow pang that hit her stomach and drained her legs of energy, and allowed her gaze to rest on his face for a few moments. He looked tired tonight, though immaculately dressed as usual in dark, form-fitting pants and a silver-grey shirt beneath the suede jacket Patti had seen before.

She noticed a lean, firm hand go to the dark hair that gleamed with reddish lights and rumple it abstractedly, giving him a careless outdoor look that reminded her too strongly of their day out riding. It was so recent, just last

Sunday, but it seemed much further in the past than that, and somehow Angus looked as though he had lived through a lot since then too. Perhaps he had had a difficult week of surgery, or maybe he had been trying to fit in too much time with Marianne . . .

Angus was looking into the crowd of bodies, now moving again in an up-to-the-minute dance tempo. He was obviously searching for someone to talk to or dance with. Patti doubted that there would be many people in the room whom he knew, and wondered if he had been brought here on sufferance by his housemen friends, who were more happy to seek their social pleasures indiscriminately, even among lowly gatherings of nurses and orderlies.

At that moment their eyes met across the crowd of heads. For what seemed like several seconds but was probably much less, his gaze locked on hers, seeming cold and indifferent, while she felt that her own expression was full of longing and hunger and that her hotly flushing cheeks probably gave away the entire secret of her feelings.

Finally she pulled her head away and focused deliberately in the opposite direction, thankful that at that moment Celine appeared only a few feet away and began to talk in her usual lively and heavily gestured way.

I won't let Angus get close to me, Patti thought desperately, then almost laughed inside. As if that would be his aim! He was probably as anxious to avoid her as she was to stay away from him.

Still, she would have to be careful that chance did not bring them together.

After Celine had touched Patti's arm in farewell and squeezed her way through the press of people to chat to

another friend, Patti went to the drinks table and absent-
ly poured herself more punch. She was feeling a little
light-headed and suspected that the fruity, sweet taste of
the drink was probably deceptive. What did people put
in punch? Vodka? Brandy? She couldn't think.

A pleasant-faced orderly whom Patti knew slightly
from her months on Jackson Ward, tapped her on the
shoulder and suggested that they dance. A set of slower
numbers were being played on the cassette player now,
and many couples were taking the opportunity of enjoying closer contact, while other people had spilled out
into the corridor and various adjoining spaces in order to
be able to converse more quietly.

Patti agreed to Chris's invitation and they swayed a
little awkwardly around a few square yards of floor,
laughing at their own clumsiness.

'I've never learnt any proper movements for this sort
of thing,' Chris confessed, and Patti nodded.

'I know. I just go from foot to foot in a sort of circle.
It's a bit silly, isn't it?'

'Nice with you,' Chris said hesitantly.

'Thank you, and with you,' Patti rejoined politely.

'You're being generous. I can't even manage the
circling part.'

'But you haven't stepped on my feet, and that's a big
plus,' Patti laughed.

The piece was fading slowly away and there was a tiny
hiatus before the next song started. Patti had forgotten
to keep her eye on Dr Pritchard's movements, so it was a
shock to find him standing right at her side and looking
down at her.

'May I have the next one?' he said in a low voice.

Patti turned a pleading eye to Chris, trying to signal
that she would rather stay with him, but he had stepped

back a few paces as if he thought that the surgeon had
some greater claim on her, and she could not meet his
eyes.

'Just a short one,' she agreed, turning back to Angus
after deciding that acceptance was the best course.

Probably he was only asking out of politeness and
would be well-satisfied with a short, dutiful turn around
the floor himself.

The first notes of a slow love-ballad sounded and Patti
saw at the edge of her vision several couples beginning to
hold each other more closely still, obviously pleased that
the music gave them the excuse to do this. Angus laid
one casual arm on her shoulder and the other fastened
around her waist, as though positioned there by the
instructor at a ballroom-dancing class. As Patti had
suspected, this was to be a purely technical exercise.

She looked up at him, daring him to guess what she
was feeling under the neat, expressionless mask into
which she had managed to compose her features. He
smiled, a quick, crooked movement that shot a pain of
longing through her.

'Tired?' he enquired, interpreting the sudden stiffening of her limbs and falling of her face as the expression
of weariness.

'Yes, I worked today—my last shift on Milsom Ward.'

'I'll be seeing you here and there in Theatre wing,
then,' he said, leaning closer towards her to speak above
the noise that was beginning to swell again.

'Yes, I suppose so.'

His comment reminded Patti of what Sister Taylor
had said on Wednesday—that it had been partly his
recommendation which had got her a place as junior
nurse in Theatre. She ought to thank him, but did not
want to do so yet. She was feeling so tongue-tied in his

presence, her body undermining her confidence with him by its draining weakness.

Almost imperceptibly he was beginning to hold her more closely as more couples moved on to the floor and the space became confined once again. Someone turned off some of the lights, creating pools of dimness here and there and leaving much of Angus's face in shadow as they turned slowly. Patti knew that she should be resisting the pull that eased her further into his arms. She should be stiffening, signalling without words that nothing had changed since the abrupt end to their kiss on Sunday and her heated words, but this feeling was simply too nice.

Foolishly she revived dreams that she had resolutely suppressed all week, thinking of how it might be in some ideal world where there was no Marianne Moore and where Angus did not think that she, Patience, was a shallow girl who could be flattered and won over by a couple of expert kisses. A world where she had the right to nestle her head against his chest like this and feel the steady beat of his heart and the movement of his breathing beneath the smooth, musk-scented silk of his shirt . . .

The slow number finished and, as if with malicious deliberation, the next piece that came on to the miscellaneous dance-music tape that Janice had prepared was a hard, fast rock song. At the same time an anonymous hand switched on the lights again, breaking Patti's melting mood with a suddenness that was like a slap in the face.

Angus seemed startled too, and the smile that crinkled around his eyes and curved his firm lips was slightly uncertain. Probably he was wondering how he could take his leave of her quickly without seeming rude.

Perhaps he had not expected her to respond to him so strongly; in fact Patti had not expected it herself and had been embarrassed and taken aback.

Patti imagined that during the week, safely back with Marianne, Angus would have looked upon Sunday's kiss as a hideous mistake, and would have been glad that her own anger and apparent rejection had eased him out of the situation. Now would he guess the truth about how much she wanted him? He had better not, and it was up to her to see that he didn't.

'Well . . . thank you for the dance,' she said. 'I can see some more people I should talk to now, though. I'm one of the guests of honour at this party, you see, so I have to spread myself around.'

Her explanation was accompanied by a thin, brittle laugh, and she noticed that Angus's reaction to it came in the form of a frown. Then he spoke.

'Yes, I won't be staying much longer, actually. I came with a couple of friends, but I've lost track of them and I don't know many other people. I'm rather tired as well . . . However, I gather that this is a belated birthday celebration for you?'

'Yes, and for one of my nursing friends, Lisa. Hers is next week and mine was three weeks ago.'

'I must wish you happy birthday then.'

'Thank you.'

'You're . . . what is it? Twenty-one?'

'Yes.' After all this time he was still unsure of her age!

He was just about to go when Patti remembered the other thing she had to thank him for.

'Sister Taylor told me on Wednesday that it was you who recommended me for Theatre.'

Her words made him turn back from the step he had already taken away from her. Probably the expression of

gratitude would bore him, but politeness demanded it
nonetheless.

'Yes,' he acknowledged. 'But I presumed she would
treat the fact as confidential.' He seemed annoyed, but
Patti pressed on.

'I'm glad she told me, because I want to thank you.'

'Don't. You're showing promise as a nurse, and I
knew you were interested in that area. I mentioned it to
Sister Taylor one day when I saw her, that's all.'

'Well . . . thank you anyway.'

'The best way you can thank me is to avoid mentioning
it to anyone. I hope you realise why.' His tone was
definitely very cool now and he had turned and was
beginning to push his way firmly through the press of
people, without having said any form of goodbye, before
she could reply to those last words of his.

Not mention it! Did he really think that she would,
after all that had passed between them now? Their first
awkward encounters, then the surprising and brief
sparking of warmth that had happened recently . . .
Both were equally good if very different reasons for
saying nothing about his recommendation.

But he had thought it necessary to turn her thanks into
this messy and unfinished scene . . .

She looked across the room to the doorway, feeling
hot with impotent anger. Was it directed against him?
Partly—but partly also at herself, and just at life. Why
could things never be tidy? There he was, disappearing
now out of the smoke haze that filled the common room
and into the clearer corridor, and then into the cool fresh
space of the night.

If he hadn't turned up so unexpectedly this evening
their relationship might have felt rounded off—not
rounded off pleasantly, but with a definite end, nonethe-

less. They could have related to each other in the
businesslike and focused atmosphere of Theatre as auto-
matons, as two people different from those who had
stood together in the corridor on Sunday night. Now it
would be harder to do that, but Patti supposed that she
would eventually learn how.

Standing there awkwardly in the middle of the room,
she started to be aware of how stuffy and unpleasant it
was becoming. People were obviously having a good
time, but the smoke from cigarettes was pricking and
stinging her eyes and the air was stale with a mingling of
heavy party smells. It seemed that there were more
strangers here now, too, and Janice and Lisa seemed to
have temporarily disappeared.

With difficulty, Patti threaded and elbowed her way
out of the room and went outside, revelling in the
spring-scented chill of the air. In the car-park next to the
nurses' home a car started up with controlled spurts
of noise. Patti recognised the sound of Angus's
Rover. Somehow it had fixed itself quite strongly in
her mind, although memorising the sounds of particular car engines was not something she normally
did.

For once the capable surgeon did not observe the low
speed limit in the hospital grounds. No other cars were
about, and Patti easily managed to follow the red tail-
lights speeding along the driveway and turning left into
the open streets. She stayed leaning against the cold
cement surface of a lamppost, listening to the noise of
the car until it faded and mingled with the general sound
of the late-night traffic.

Angus was gone—home, perhaps, or to the flat in
Belgravia where, it seemed, Marianne Moore lived.

'Not enjoying the party?' a young man said lightly as

he walked past hand in hand with a second-year nurse on their way to a car.

Neither of them expected a reply and Patti had none to give. Her thoughts were where they should not be—with Angus—but for the moment she didn't seem to be able to do anything about it.

'Here you are! We've been looking for you everywhere!' Janice exclaimed. 'We're going to have the cake.'

'A cake? You shouldn't have!' Patti said, trying to be enthusiastic.

'Of course we had to have one. So come on before everybody loses interest again and goes back to dancing.'

Janice pulled Patti towards the door, then spoke again.

'By the way, did you see Dr Pritchard? I invited him specially because I thought you'd like me to, and I thought I caught a glimpse of him, but I can't seem to find him now.'

'I saw him. He's just left,' Patti said.

CHAPTER TEN

'THAT WILL do, I think,' Dr Thomas said, stepping back and straightening up from the inert form of the woman on the operating table.

After two weeks in theatre, Patience had come to expect the words from this slightly stooped, grey-haired man in his middle fifties. Every surgeon had his own particular mannerism of speech or action. Some were amusing, others a little annoying, but each was as much a part of that surgeon's technique as the way an incision was made or gloves were put on.

Patti liked Dr Thomas. His calm, precise way of working helped to create an atmosphere of alertness but not destructive tension. The middle-aged woman, who was now being taken to the recovery ward, had been undergoing the routine removal of a cyst, but no one treated the operation any less seriously than if it had been a major piece of transplant surgery.

Patti looked about her as she helped the scrub nurse prepare for the arrival of the next patient by laying out sterile packs of instruments and dressings.

The atmosphere of the theatre, so strange and awe-inspiring at first, was beginning to seem far less frightening now. She had become used to the ever-present lights, to the lack of windows, and to the rigorous vigilance about sterility. A slight draining of her strength when she had to stand close to a patient after a major incision had been made had faded almost completely now too, and had been replaced by a strong interest in every facet of the procedure of surgery, from the moment the patient was first wheeled in and transferred to the flat, board-like table, to the time when the nurses in the recovery ward took over.

The feeling of being part of a team seemed stronger to her here than it had been on Jackson and Milsom wards. The communication between anaesthetist and surgeon and between surgeon and nurse was often terse, as there was seldom time for wasted words here, but understanding was usually immediate, and only very occasionally did an instruction or comment have to be repeated.

As yet, of course, Patti was only the trainee, the most junior part of this team, scarcely noticed unless she made a mistake or was too slow, in which case she would earn an irritated glance from the surgeon or would hear an added note of impatience in the other nurse's tone.

After such incidents had happened twice on her first day, Patti had felt depressed, thinking that this boded ill for her ambitions to be a qualified sister in Theatre, but the senior nurse on her shift, an older and very capable woman named Margaret Curtis, had noticed Patti's frown of tension and apprehension.

'Don't dwell on the times when a surgeon speaks sharply to you,' Sister Curtis had advised. 'It's not personal, and it does not mean you are slow or inefficient. We all have to keep on our toes in something as important as this, and there is no time for polite waiting. If Dr Thomas thinks that you haven't heard, or have misunderstood, he is going to make sure that the second time there is no room for doubt.'

'I do feel jumpy when it happens though,' Patti had confessed.

'Try not to,' Sister Curtis advised. 'Try to use your

jumpiness in a positive way. Let it help you to be even quicker and more alert, and soon you will find you are anticipating Dr Thomas's instructions, and my own, before they are even given.'

Patti was learning to accept this and, as often happens, she found that she worked faster and made less mistakes now that she felt that an occasional slowness did not matter. She was always at the surgeon's side ready to tie the pieces of tape at the back of his traditional green gown and no longer feared that she would accidentally trespass on one of the sterile fields in the operating area with her own ungloved and non-sterile fingers.

But of course, the grey-haired senior surgeon was not the only one with whom Patience came into contact. There was Dr Teasdell, whom she had known on Jackson Ward, Dr Llewellyn, whom she remembered Alison Reed referring to as 'delicious', and, of course, Angus Pritchard.

Patti never knew in advance if she would encounter him during a particular day. Each of the hospital's theatres specialised in a particular area of surgery and had special equipment to match that function. Patti moved from theatre to theatre, sometimes in the field of ophthalmic surgery, sometimes dealing with orthopaedic cases and so on, and even if she was rostered on to Theatre D, where Angus Pritchard was usually to be found, she did not know if he would be performing surgery that day or not. Conversely, if she was assigned to duty in another theatre, she still ran the risk of encountering him in a corridor, during a tea-break, or in one of the auxiliary spaces that serviced the theatres themselves.

In the twelve days that had passed since the party, Angus had remained in her thoughts as a depressing and disturbing presence. Physically, her awareness of him seemed to be indelibly imprinted on her senses. Constantly, at unexpected times, an image of him would flash across her mind's eye—a gesture that he made often, the shape of his capable shoulders, the movement of his smile.

She could not forget the awkwardness of that last conversation and the humiliation of finding out that Janice had actually asked him specially to the party, thinking that Patti would be pleased. It had been hard to accept that Angus's very presence at the party had been inspired out of duty and politeness. Of course, Patti had told herself, when he had asked her to dance that this was just a gesture on his part; but somewhere inside her she had not really believed it and had allowed her body to seduce itself into thinking that the dance was important. But Janice's words had made her realise the truth in a way that could not be ignored.

After going back inside with Janice, Patti had performed the cake-cutting ceremony with Lisa with a show of pleasure that had pleased everyone, and then she had stayed for a further hour, hiding her feelings and joining in the lively atmosphere. The next day they had all helped to clean up. It turned out that nothing had been broken, and Sister Clayton and the rest of the staff of the nurses' home seemed pleased with the whole event, not to mention many other people who came up to Patti in the dining-hall over the next few days to tell her how much they had enjoyed themselves.

When Patti saw Angus Pritchard he did not refer to the party at all. In fact they barely spoke. He said hallo to her when they passed each other in a corridor, he gave her instructions as he would do to any nurse, and once he had said casually, 'Enjoying Theatre?' and had nodded uninterestedly, it seemed to Patience, at her affirmative reply.

She thought about all this as she prepared for Dr Thomas's next patient on this Thursday, her ninth day of work in Theatre. In fact, at any time when her thoughts did not have to be busy elsewhere, they always returned to this painful point. It was so different from how she yearned for it to be.

There could be so much to exchange with Angus if only they were communicating as they had done on that golden weekend at Wellham. There were so many questions she would have asked him about his work, now that she was beginning to understand and be interested in it so much more. But it seemed as though they might never talk in a real way to each other again.

The next day, Friday, she was assigned to duty in Theatre D. Work began there at half-past eight, with preparatory tasks being done by nurses, ready for the arrival of surgeon, assistant surgeon and anaesthetist, and finally the patient.

'Could you check through this tray of dirty instruments, please, Nurse Rainer,' Sister Curtis said, just as Patti was beginning to feel the familiar tension as she wondered whether it would be Dr Pritchard who was working in here today.

Before she had finished the task, she was aware that he had entered the room.

'I'm ready to be scrubbed, up, Sister,' he said to Margaret Curtis, flashing a quick, unreadable glance at Patti, but not acknowledging the faint nod and smile she gave him.

She turned back to her work feeling hot and uncertain. Was she expected to act as if they did not even know each other now?

'You're going on holiday next week, aren't you, Margaret?' he was saying now to Sister Curtis in a pleasant, conversational way.

'Yes, my husband has to go to Rome on business so we are combining the trip with three weeks of exploring Italy,' Sister Curtis replied with happy anticipation in her voice, and the two continued to discuss the delights of a holiday in Rome while the procedure of scrubbing and putting on cap, mask and sterile gloves was completed.

Patti had nothing to do for these few moments, so she found it impossible not to spend the time looking surreptitiously at Angus, although the way he was turned away from her seemed deliberate in its coldness.

He still looked tired, Patti thought. His face was paler than she had ever seen it. Obviously none of the outdoor activities or trips away that had kept it tanned almost the whole time she had known him were being fitted into his schedule at the moment . . .

A few minutes later everything was ready and the patient was on his way from the anaesthetist's room. This morning's operation would be a long and difficult one, testing Angus Pritchard's skills to a great extent and providing Patti with the opportunity to witness more advanced and delicate surgery than she had yet seen.

David Brace was a young mechanic who had suffered bad burns in an accident at work. At one time it had been thought that his left arm would have to be amputated below the elbow, but the work of the staff in the burns unit and the patient's own positive attitude to his recovery over a period of months had meant that the arm was saved, although much mobility in the hand had been lost.

The case was similar in many ways to that of Glenn

Baker, whom Patti still remembered well from her days on Jackson Ward, but today the patient was receiving treatment not to his face but to his damaged arm.

New techniques in which Angus Pritchard was intensely interested made it possible for three fingers of the hand to be reconstructed out of tissue taken from the groin. Special pressure bandages worn for many months would reduce the incidence and severity of scarring. The fingers would never be fully functional and would not be able to move independently of each other, but with David Brace's thumb and forefinger still able to oppose each other, he would be able to pick up objects within a certain size range.

The functional success of the hand would directly depend on how Dr Pritchard performed today, and Patti could see as she stood back, waiting alertly for instructions from Sister Curtis, that the surgeon was more tense than usual, building himself into a state of completely focused concentration.

The anaesthetist was alert and ready too, monitoring the patient's level of unconsciousness constantly on the complicated equipment with which he was so familiar.

Angus began by checking the preparations made to the area from which the skin graft was to be taken. Then the operation began in earnest and the minutes ticked by completely unnoticed by Patti, who could think of nothing but the space in which she stood and the events that were going on.

Today she did not need to be told anything twice. Angus Pritchard became the centre of her world and, even though she often did not fully understand the things he was doing, some other kind of knowledge took over, so that when he murmured a word to Sister Curtis, who in turn issued an instruction to another nurse and thence to Patience, the order was never unexpected.

There were lulls, of course—periods of time when Patti simply stood watching, while Angus's fingers performed tasks that seemed much too delicate for their size and length. During those times she could not forget what he meant to her, and how every gesture he made was dear.

His rich chestnut hair was hidden today beneath a cap, and most of his face was covered by a green mask, but his eyes were enough of a reminder of how unuterrably attractive she found him. They seemed greener than usual in the unnatural light of the theatre, mostly staring down at his work, but occasionally looking up towards the assistant surgeon or towards Sister Curtis. And once or twice they cut sharply across to Patti herself, resting on her face only for a moment, but piercing her with a pang of longing in just that short time.

'How am I going to be able to bear three months of this!' she thought, not believing any more that she would be able to squash the love she felt for him within a few weeks of resolute effort.

After what seemed like hours, the final stitches had been threaded in and the last perfect and delicate dressings fixed into place. David Brace was then transferred to a trolley and wheeled away to the recovery ward.

Dr Pritchard peeled off gloves, cap and mask as he walked away from the table over which his attention had been focused, and signalled a brief, anonymous indication to Patti that she should help him to remove the soiled green gown.

She hurried over and willed her fingers to be quick and steady as she untied the tape ties that fastened the gown at the back. One of them had become pulled into a tight knot and she could not manage to loosen it for what seemed like minutes, nerving herself every second for impatient words from him. But he did not speak, standing silently and stiffly as if this annoyance was a regular part of the routine and he had learned to accept it.

Finally the knot was picked loose and he dragged the sleeves of the gown down his long arms with a very evident sigh of relief. Standing close to him, Patti could see a dew of sweat on his forehead and a few small curls of hair clinging damply there. He screwed his face up for a moment in a grimace, as though stretching out muscles stiffened from tension, then ran a finger around the neck of the clean white T-shirt which all surgeons wore under their gowns.

On an impulse, Patti picked up a thick dry towel that lay folded on a nearby shelf and held it out to him. For a moment he stood there without taking it, simply relaxing, and Patti felt foolish with one hand stuck out towards him. She was about to put the towel down again and turn away to hide her embarrassment by finding some tiny unnecessary task to perform, when he reached a hand out for it at last and buried his face in its soft folds, obviously relishing the sensation.

Patti would have been happy to stay near him like this, watching him and enjoying each movement he made, but it would have been ridiculous so she stepped away and looked for something else to put her mind to. She felt hot herself in the neat but rather stiff white uniform, and being so close to Angus Pritchard scarcely increased her comfort.

'You should go in for morning coffee now, Patience,' Sister Curtis said briskly, finishing certain post-operative procedures for which she was responsible as she spoke. 'I'll be along to the rest room in about five minutes, but we haven't got too much time this morning. There's another patient to fit in before lunch, and that last one was so long.'

Patti nodded, then turned too quickly, and the room with its staring lights suddenly spun round horribly, while the floor seemed to be sliding up to meet her as she stepped unsteadily forward.

'Hold on!' Angus Pritchard caught her expertly, saving her from a series of ungainly staggering steps, if not from actually falling.

For several seconds Patti could not stop herself from leaning heavily against him, still feeling that the blood was draining dizzily from her head and that she needed some support while she breathed deeply a few times. The giddy feeling had been very unexpected. She had not realised how much the intense concentration of the past few hours had tired her and felt that Angus must think she was very weak and spineless to be so affected by it.

'Sorry,' she said. 'I'm all right now.'

'No, you're not,' Angus said firmly. 'Keep breathing deeply and don't try to let go of me just yet.'

'Really, I can . . .' She stopped, unable to finish the sentence.

His hands on her arm and her waist made her think back to some of the things he had done that morning. She saw again the clean slices of skin coming away and leaving raw red planes on David Brace's body . . .

'The skin graft and reconstruction?' Angus queried gently, seeming to guess exactly what Patti was seeing in her mind's eye.

'Yes, I'm sorry, I . . .'

'It's all right. Everybody feels it at first. And that process is not terribly pretty. You think you've overcome your squeamishness, but a long operation like that can sometimes bring it back again. And you've been standing up for quite a while this morning. I'll take you into the tea-room.'

He was leading Patti there gently as he spoke and she gave up the idea of trying to protest further. It was so inexpressibly nice to feel the warm support of his body against hers as they walked, and to hear him speak to her in the soft tones she hadn't dared to imagine him using to her again. It was only because the incident aroused his instincts as a doctor, of course. She sighed.

'Feeling better?'

'Yes, thank you.'

The words would probably make him let her go but she couldn't lie about it just so that he would keep holding her. Strength *was* returning now and she felt quite able to stand alone, but his hold on her did not loosen and a moment later he had set her down in one of the comfortable armchairs of the tea-room. Then he was on his way to prepare her coffee himself, greeting a couple of colleagues as he passed their chairs.

He returned with the hot brew a few minutes later, as well as carrying a cup for himself, and sat in the chair next to hers, although she was sure he would rather have gone to the window-side group of seats where his fellow surgeons sat. Patti wanted to say this to him but did not dare. Very likely he would be embarrassed and angry if the distance that existed between them now was acknowledged explicitly in words.

'Do you feel recovered completely?' he asked.

'Yes, thank you, I do. And I am sorry about all this,' she replied. 'I'm surprised that I felt faint and I'm sure I won't again. You're the one who has the most right to feel faint and tired.'

'I do,' he admitted. 'But I'm used to it, and I'm sure you will be all right from now on.'

He put an absent hand to his neck and felt the towel that still hung there forgotten, giving him a careless, athletic look.

'I'll take that for you,' Patti put in quickly as he removed it, looking a little irritated as he did so.

He handed it to her without a word and she folded it, laying it on a little table while she finished her coffee. Angus had sunk back into his chair now, and was evidently not going to try to make further conversation with her. He was probably already thinking of the next operation and what it would require of him.

The rest of the day passed uneventfully, with Angus once more seeming to forget that Patti was someone he knew outside the different world that was Theatre. Patti thought that no one who saw them working together would ever have guessed that in fact he had kissed her twice, and kissed her long and fully . . .

She had a normal weekend off, because as many as possible of the non-urgent operations were performed during weekday, day-time hours. As usually happened every few weekends, her father collected her at six after she had had time to shower, change and prepare a weekend bag, and took her down to Wellham.

It was good to be home and able to feel free and relaxed again, with time spent in family doings as well as riding Becky for several hours each day. This was the first time Patti had been home since the weekend when Angus had come down—now three weeks ago, although it seemed in many ways so much longer. Things and people seemed to be conspiring to remind her of that too-lovely time—the weather was similarly gorgeous, and inevitably her riding took her along some of the same paths she had travelled with Angus—so she found that the weekend did not end up being as complete a break from hospital concerns as she had hoped.

'You must tell Angus how much we enjoyed having him down here,' Mrs Rainer said to Patti as they washed the supper dishes together on Saturday night. 'We'd lost touch a bit while the boys were little and took so much of my time, but now I think we're renewing the friendship, and I like him so much.'

'Do you? That's good,' Patti replied mechanically, staring too earnestly at the plate she was wiping and hoping that the blush she felt on her cheeks didn't show too much.

'Yes, and your father agrees. We want to have him down again soon, if he'd like to come. I meant to write him a note about it, but what with the fête at the boys' school, I haven't had time. Do you think you could mention it to him for me when you see him in the operating theatre? I know you said you don't see very much of him at the hospital as it might create bad feeling, but surely that would be possible?'

'Perhaps not actually in the operating theatre,' Patti said, smiling a little bitterly at the picture her mind sketched out—last Friday's long, tense surgery inter-rupted by the student nurse passing on a message from her mother. 'But I'll try to some other time.'

'Good, because you seem to get on well with him, too. Don't you?'

'I suppose so.'

'You like him, I can tell. And I'm sure he likes you.'

'Yes, perhaps.'

What on earth could she reply if her mother started probing more deeply into her feelings for Angus? It was very fortunate that at that moment Christopher stomped noisily into the kitchen to pour himself a glass of milk, and any intimate mother-daughter conversation was precluded.

But it wouldn't be possible for Patti to go on trying to avoid the subject of Angus Pritchard indefinitely, with her mother or anyone else.

She went back to the hospital on Sunday night, not looking forward to tomorrow's shift on Theatre F very much at all. If she met Angus in the corridor of theatre wing, or in the tea-room, would she pass on her mother's message? Or should she ring the surgeon especially, in order to remove the thing from the world of the hospital altogether?

She didn't decide either way, feeling that she could afford to procrastinate for a few days at least, and wishing that there was some way Angus could be taken out of her life completely for a long period. Couldn't he receive an invitation to lecture on micro-surgical techniques in New Zealand for eighteen months, or something?

The operations scheduled for Theatre F that day were all fairly routine, although it was the biggest and best-equipped of all the theatres at the Sir Richard Gregory Memorial Hospital. This was the first time that Patti had been assigned to work here and she soon found herself caught up in a fascination for the efficiency of the technology and techniques she saw. Most of what could be done in this theatre was not demonstrated that morning, but Patti knew that its location and fittings equipped it for use in the most dramatic of emergency surgery when required. Lisa sat with her at lunch and they talked about the place together.

'I hadn't thought much about Theatre till you started

working there,' Patti's dark-haired friend said. 'But now I'm quite looking forward to my turn there, even though it probably won't come until late next year—or even until the third year.'

'Are you enjoying it as much as you expected to?' another first-year nurse, Suzanne, asked.

'Some parts of it more than I thought I would, and other parts less,' Patti said, not wanting to go into details about what those other parts were. Fortunately Lisa was still following a track of her own.

'I'm finding it so interesting to think of receiving patients that you have just been dealing with, Patti,' she said. 'Although we don't get to find out too much about them in Recovery.'

Suzanne asked a couple of questions about work in the recovery ward, then there was a little lull while they tackled their hot, energy-giving meal. But before Patti had finished it, a paging announcement echoed through the dining-hall.

These were often being made, although most doctors carried their own electronic bleeper as well, and Patti had grown too used to them, without having any expectation that one might be for her, to pay much attention. In fact, the name that the woman's voice called this time didn't register with her at all.

Lisa was the one who heard it.

'Patti, they've just paged you!'

'I beg your pardon?'

'That paging announcement was for you. You're to go back on duty straight away.'

Patti came to herself at once, following instructions that had been stressed during their initial training period. If you were called, you went—without waiting to ask why, or to finish what you had been doing. Patti left

Lisa and Suzanne to make interested speculations about what the nature of the emergency could be.

The distance between the dining-hall and the theatre wing could take several minutes to cover at a leisurely or tired pace, but if you ran, as Patti was now doing, it did not take long at all. Although she had no idea of what atmosphere she would find in Theatre F, Patti guessed that she was being called back to act as scout for some kind of urgent operation, probably a patient still on their way by ambulance after an accident.

Sister Bellamy, a pleasant-faced, ash-blonde nurse in her late twenties who was sponge nurse in Theatre F that day, was waiting for Patience as she hurried into the annexe that opened off the operating room.

'You hadn't finished your lunch, I suppose?'

'No.'

'Well, let's hope you're not tired and are feeling a little rested anyway, because we have something very long and difficult coming up. There's an ambulance on its way here with a six-year-old girl. She has had four fingers on her right hand severed by a butcher's slicer.'

Sister Bellamy put out a hand to press Patti's shoulder in response to her instinctive gasp of horror, reminding the junior nurse that she could not let such feelings affect her at a time like this. Then she continued.

'Both the mother and the butcher were very quick and cool. They've saved the fingers using ice from the freezer in the shop and her poor little hand is being protected as well as it can be, too. They expect to be here in about ten minutes, and there's a very good chance, these days, that the fingers can be re-attached . . . But it will be a long operation—six or seven hours. I was very pleased with the way you worked this morning, but you'll have to be prepared to feel quite exhausted at the end of this.'

'I had the weekend off, and I'm still feeling fresh,' Patti said, infected by the drama of the situation. She was nervous, but this would be the most dramatic thing she had yet been involved in, and one part of her was rising to the challenge of it already.

The two nurses spent the next few minutes making absolutely certain that everything was in readiness, then there was a stirring of activity as the footsteps of the three surgeons who would perform the infinitely delicate work on the little girl's hand could be heard coming rapidly along the corridor.

First came a distinguished-looking man whom Patti did not recognise, then an assistant surgeon with whom she had worked before. The last man to enter was Angus Pritchard.

This should not have been a shock, but it was. Patti had been too busy digesting the information about the afternoon that lay ahead to realise that of course Dr Pritchard, with his interest and knowledge in this field, would be involved in the operation.

He strode to the scrubbing-up area without so much as tossing a glance in her direction. In fact she thought that very possibly he had not seen her, for he was exchanging earnest words with the third surgeon. He was speaking rapidly and seemed tense. Patti guessed that perhaps the third unknown surgeon was someone important and that, quite apart from the test of saving the child's hand, which was something Angus Pritchard would feel he had to pass, there was another test as well. Because after all, Angus was still young for the position in which he found himself. The way he performed in front of the grey-haired stranger, whose quiet, authoritative words came with a strong American accent, could have a major effect on the future of his career.

It was only towards the end of the scrubbing-up procedure that Patience stepped forward to tie the tabs at the back of the gowns of the three men, and it was as she finished this that Angus turned and registered her presence at last.

'You're part of this team?' he asked in a low voice that to Patti seemed filled with horror.

'Y-yes,' she stammered, adding unnecessarily, 'I'm scouting.'

'You can't!' The words were quite fierce.

He turned around and saw that the other four people were involved in final preparations and were not aware of the tense interchange that was in progress.

Part of Patti's mind registered the first faint howls of the ambulance siren, growing louder and closer by the second, but more of her attention was riveted on Angus. What did he mean, she couldn't? What was he going to do?

'I'm sorry, I don't understand,' she said, trembling now. He looked so angry.

'I mean I can't have you here, you of all people, the way I feel about . . . Not at this operation.'

CHAPTER ELEVEN

FOR A second Angus stood there as if waiting for Patti to act. His eyes were fixed on her face and colder, she thought, than they had ever been before. What did he want her to say? That she felt ill and couldn't go on? All right then, even if it destroyed any trust people had in her here in Theatre. Perhaps she could say something like that, if he was serious . . .

Another look at Angus's face told Patti that he was. Whatever comments and last-minute action it caused, he was not going to have her take part in the operation. He took a step forward and for a moment Patti thought that he was going to push her physically from the room, but then he turned to the others, not acknowledging the greeting of the anaesthetist who had just arrived.

'I'm sorry, but there will have to be a change before we can start. We can't have this girl act as scout. She wouldn't be able to handle it. She collapsed last Friday during surgery. Sister Bellamy, can you make other arrangements?'

At that moment the ambulance pulled up in the nearby bay and Patti heard voices as the stretcher was passed out.

'Nurse Brown will scout here,' Sister Bellamy said quickly after darting a surprised glance at Angus and Patti. 'Nurse Rainer, go to Theatre G and explain what has happened. You will take over there as scout.' As Patti left the dramatic atmosphere of Theatre F, the little girl was brought in.

178

The afternoon seemed very long to Patti, although she resolutely refused to allow any organised thoughts about what had just occurred to disturb her concentration on the four routine pieces of surgery with which she assisted in Theatre G. The arrangement of the theatres, with its emphasis on sterility and on creating separate, efficient and autonomous working units, meant that no sound at all filtered between the spaces. When Patti left the theatre wing at the end of her shift, her hands shaking suddenly now that she could allow them to, she knew that the drama would still be going on in Theatre F, but no sign of that could be seen from outside.

She tried to tell herself that what had happened did not matter, that it was the saving of life and limb that was important, not her own feelings. If Angus had truly felt that she was incompetent, then he could only have acted as he had done.

But in fact she knew that it was more than simply an objective assessment of her worth as a nurse that had made him ask her to leave. It was a deeply felt personal dislike of her that, when she thought about it, always seemed to have been there as an undercurrent in their relationship. The weekend spent at her parents' had been something apart from that. Something in the atmosphere had seduced him temporarily into forgetting what he really felt about her. That could happen very easily, and did to many people.

And Friday's apparent concern over her dizziness would not have been hard to feign for a doctor, who must have a warm, impartial bedside manner towards everyone.

But it was today's incident that told her once again, and very finally, that he disliked her intensely now. She could not forget the horrified disbelief that had filled his features when he had seen her. He was very tense about the operation and simply did not have the time or energy to hide what he felt. 'I can't have you here, you of all people,' he had said in a voice that was drained of all expression . . .

Patti had been walking along almost blindly as she thought all this, her footsteps taking her automatically to the nurses' home. As she passed through the foyer she looked across at the magazine table, a gesture that, quite against her will, had become automatic now.

And the magazine was there! She recognised the glossily-printed, smiling face on the cover, and the bold yellow of the caption straight away. Someone had obviously finished it and had dropped it back on the table sometime today. It was looking a little the worse for wear, but was still only four weeks old. Patti went over to the table, knowing that the story of Marianne Moore's success in work and love could only depress her, but deciding that she felt so miserable already that it didn't matter.

The magazine was a recently-begun television and film gossip weekly, boldly and colourfully printed, but not of a very high quality. Patti flipped through several pages of show business news, rumour and scandal before she found the story about Marianne.

It was illustrated with several more pictures—three of just Marianne herself, dressed each time in a different and beautiful fashion creation, and a fourth showing her in what must be one of her period costumes from the film, with a boldly good-looking dark-haired man holding her closely. Presumably he was her co-star and this was a publicity still for *Silver Wind*, which was soon to be released.

Patti glanced down at the caption beneath this photo.

Marianne and Damon in Silver Wind—*love blossomed off set as well as on.*

She dropped the magazine. What was this story saying? That the lover Marianne was returning to was not Angus Pritchard at all?

She skimmed through the cliché-ridden text. *Lovely new star . . . up-and-coming English actor Damon Tyler . . . met on the set of Peter Eckermann's new film . . . 'It was practically love at first sight,' confesses Marianne.* But the couple had to be parted for several weeks when Damon was due back in London for work in a new television drama, and Marianne was still needed in California for re-takes. *'I missed her so much that I just rang her up one day and proposed,' Damon says. 'And I accepted straight away,' Marianne adds, 'although it was two o'clock in the morning where I was!'*

The article continued for a few more frothy paragraphs, and Patti read them quickly, without taking everything in.

So much seemed different now, and yet nothing was, really. At first, when she had realised that Marianne was no longer involved with Angus, Patti had felt a surging of hope. This must mean that when the phone had rung interrupting their first kiss, and it had been Marianne, she had only been ringing out of friendship. Angus had not gone straight to a romantic meeting with her . . .

But then Patti's thoughts became more realistic once again. Angus was not in love with Marianne, but that changed nothing about his feelings for herself. Today's scene in Theatre F had proved that, and in fact she probably ought to feel more depressed after finding out the truth about Marianne's love than she had before.

It was easy to see that Marianne's sudden romance might have hurt Angus. He had probably known about its blossoming before his return from America, and that kiss in his flat was just an attempt to forget the lovely actress through the distraction of a light flirtation, or even an affair, with a pretty little nurse who insisted on forcing herself into his path, even though he had no respect for her.

My thoughts are just going round and round stupidly, Patti realised, putting the magazine back on the table where a few others were scattered. 'I'm behaving like a fourteen-year-old. I can't ever find out the complete truth about Angus, about those kisses, and about exactly how much he has disliked me on any particular day.'

She knew that she simply had to stop thinking about it, stop plunging into these pointless and circular guessing games, and accept that nothing could be done to salvage any friendship that might once have been possible.

Tiredly, but with squared shoulders, she went upstairs to her room and changed out of the slightly crumpled white uniform, deliberately choosing to put on bright, pretty clothes in an attempt to cheer herself up—salmon pink cotton trousers and a white cotton pullover that was brightened by a pretty floral motif in embroidery and appliqué on the front. She let her hair down too, brushing it vigorously, then shaking her head so that it fluffed out lightly all round.

There was still more than an hour to pass before tea. Patti made a cup of coffee in the kitchen annexe off the sixth floor common room, chatting for a few minutes to a couple of friends, then returned and sat at her desk working on a nursing assignment until she could go down and meet her friends.

But after the meal, which had been extended by a session of talk with Lisa and Janice, it was difficult to return to her lonely room. The others were planning to watch a television movie, she knew, and they expected her to join them, but for half an hour Patti simply lay on her bed in the dark, abandoning herself to the misery which would not go away just because she had decided that it should.

By half-past eight she had stopped the pointless indulgence in tears, but was still feeling heavy-headed and wished that the oblivion of sleep would come. But of course, it was too early.

There was a knock at the door—no doubt Lisa come to tell her that the film was starting. She got up and wiped her face quickly, then fluffed her hair around her cheeks to try to hide any traces of redness that might remain.

'I'm coming, Lisa. Just a minute. Sorry, I was just . . .'

She opened the door and came face to face with Angus Pritchard.

'I want to talk,' he said abruptly.

'Well . . . come in then,' was her confused reply. He was the last person she had expected to see, especially today, and of course his body was immediately having its usual disturbing effect on her senses.

'No, not here,' he was saying. 'Do you think I could say anything properly in the nurses' home?'

'Where then? I mean, shall I get my bag?'

'Yes, we'll go to a café.'

He turned and was striding back down the corridor to the lift, barely giving Patti time to pick up her bag, check that she had her key and lock the door behind her.

What was this all for, and why was he in such a hurry? She remembered the accusations he had made against her the first time they had gone to a café together. After today's scene in Theatre it seemed likely that tonight was going to be almost a repeat performance. Probably he would tell her that they had decided to move her to a ward for the next three months. She should have insisted on hearing him out in her room rather than going through all this.

On the way down in the lift she saw for the first time how utterly exhausted he looked, and remembered why. The operation on the child's hand! Surely . . . yes, he must only just have finished it! She saw that the smooth planes of his face were pale almost to greyness, and that the hand which pressed the door-close and ground-floor buttons of the lift was not completely steady.

'Angus!' She had used his first name, but it was too late to regret it. 'You're so tired. You should have said so and I would have made you a cup of coffee upstairs.'

'I'd prefer to get out, to get away.'

'Yes, of course. The operation—can I ask? Was it a success?'

'We don't know yet. We think so. I'd rather not talk about this afternoon just yet.'

There was a husky, forced note in his voice, and as he turned away from her towards the doors of the lift, Patti thought she saw the glint of tears in his eyes. But he was steady and sure again as they went through the foyer, both ignoring the glances of two girls who sat there. It would probably be enough to restart those ludicrous rumours that they were involved together, but that scarcely mattered to Patti right now.

Angus's car was parked outside, so they were out of the hospital grounds only a minute later, turning along the street that led to the Coffee-Pot, the café where he had first taken her. It seemed like an exact repeat of that time, with silence in the car as they drove and then a quick walk to the most private and isolated table, followed by his unhesitating order of coffees.

It was a quiet night tonight. There were only two other groups of people in another corner of the squared C-shape of the café, and the one waitress stayed by her espresso machine, so to all intents and purposes they were alone.

'I want to apologise about this afternoon,' Angus said as soon as their coffees had been brought.

Patti's heart sank. Why was he doing this? It wasn't necessary. His reaction today had betrayed the truth about how he felt and there was no need to gloss it over with polite lies.

'Don't apologise,' she said, not knowing what else to add.

'But I must. It was unpardonable and unprofessional. I'll make sure that the rest of the staff know that. Your faintness last Friday had nothing to do with it. I'm sure you realise that. I'm sure you know the real reason, and I'm sorry I had to force it upon your notice again.' He spoke in a low voice.

'The real reason? That you can't bear the sight of me? There's nothing I can . . .' She broke off as he leaned forward and interrupted her.

'Can't bear you? What are you talking about? You were the one to reject me when I kissed you . . . Can that really be what you think, that I don't like you?' He broke off, staring at her in amazement, his eyes deeply sea-toned.

Patti looked back at him, pink-cheeked and scarcely daring to believe in the warmth that she saw in his face. Then at last his meaning became unmistakable.

'Patti, my darling, I think we've both been making a terrible mistake about each other for quite a long time.'

The words were whispered by firm lips only an inch from her own—then there was no distance between them at all as he kissed her softly and lingeringly, in no hurry to complete the tender exploration of her mouth because now they both knew that there would be plenty of time for it.

'Do you really want this coffee?' he murmured a few minutes later.

'Not really.'

'Good, because I think it will be getting cold.'

'And what about yours?'

'I've lost interest in it completely. Let's go outside, shall we?'

They left the café arm in arm, oblivious of the curious glance of the waitress, and walked lazily and aimlessly for a while in the cool night.

'My darling, can you explain for me, please, why you thought that I didn't like you?'

'Oh, Angus, weren't there a dozen things? You were so cold and disapproving at first, and any time there was any friendliness I just thought you were acting out of duty to my parents.'

'Yes, perhaps that's true. But I soon realised I had been completely mistaken about you.'

'But you didn't tell me that, not in so many words.'

'Perhaps I didn't . . .' he said.

'And then I saw you out with Marianne Moore and I assumed you were in love with her. Even when we seemed to get on well—that day out riding, and when you kissed me—I thought . . . I don't know. I thought that my hopes were just naive and you were only amusing yourself.'

'Did you really believe I was like that?' he asked.

'I thought perhaps everyone was, and I was too young

to have found it out yet. I thought that perhaps there were rules you were playing by that I didn't understand, and it was all my fault.'

'I suppose there are those rules,' he admitted. 'But I wasn't playing them. I knew that weekend at your parents' that I wanted to know and love you completely, and I thought that kissing you would start to tell you that, but then you pulled away. And I didn't think you had any reason to believe I was serious about Marianne . . .'

'Were you ever serious about her?' Patti asked.

'Not really. We had a good time together for a while, but I knew I wanted something more permanent than I could ever have with her. She has already been divorced twice, and I don't expect that her marriage with Damon Tyler will last any longer than the first two did. I'm not necessarily condemning her for that, but it's not the kind of life I would want. I'm looking for someone with life, sincerity, a sense of humour and fun . . . You.' He kissed her softly.

'Damon Tyler . . . That was what really made me think you and Marianne were engaged,' Patti said. Angus looked at her in surprise.

'How?'

'I saw a magazine headline saying that Marianne Moore was flying home from Hollywood to her new love. I assumed that meant you.'

'But surely when you read the article . . . ?'

'I didn't read it. That was the trouble. I just saw the heading one night and didn't get a chance to look at the magazine then. And when I tried to find it, it had disappeared off the magazine table. I only found it again and read it properly this afternoon.'

'And you thought I didn't want you in Theatre be-

cause I couldn't stand the sight of you, when in fact it was
the exact opposite. I couldn't take my eyes off you, and I
simply couldn't afford that distraction today.'

'Well, now you can save looking at me for out of work
hours,' Patti said archly.

'I will. As long as you'll let me do that a lot, my love,'
he replied, kissing each of her eyelids and the tip of her
nose in turn.

They had returned to the car now and he had opened
the passenger door so that she could get in. Then he
came and seated himself beside her.

'I don't want you to spend all your time looking at me
when we're together,' Patti said now.

'You don't?'

'No, you're to devote a fairly high proportion of it to
kissing me.'

He responded to this hint immediately, but then
pulled gently away. 'I suppose we had better make some
plans.'

'Yes?'

'I'm asking you to marry me, you realise that, don't
you?'

'I thought you might be, but I wasn't quite sure,' Patti
confessed.

'Is it "yes"?'

'Of course . . .'

'I think we should wait for six months,' Angus said a
few moments later. 'We'll have a wonderful time, getting to know everything about each other, doing things
together. It will give you time to know your feelings
fully . . .'

'I do know them.'

'Patience my love, I'm twelve years older than you are.
I've had to work out what I want to happen in my life.

You need something of the same opportunity.'

'But . . .'

'Shh! That doesn't matter for now. But there is something I haven't told you yet. I've been asked to go to America—California—for a year starting in November, to work with Dr Casson who was at the operation today. I'm going to go, but . . . are you willing to marry me and come too?'

'I'd love to!'

A rosy vista of the future opened up in Patti's mind, and when she looked into Angus's eyes she could see it there too. They would have their honeymoon somewhere—perhaps in America, perhaps in Europe—then set up their first home together in California, working hard, seeing and experiencing new things, but above all being together.

'It will mean postponing your training for a year, and perhaps two,' Angus frowned.

'That's all right,' she assured him. 'I'll be able to find something interesting to do over there.'

'Then everything is perfect?' Angus whispered, his breath caressing her ear.

'Perfect,' she sighed, then nestled into his arms and waited for his kiss.

The perfect holiday romance.

ACT OF BETRAYAL
Sara Craven
MAN HUNT
Charlotte Lamb

YOU OWE ME
Penny Jordan
LOVERS IN THE AFTERNOON
Carole Mortimer

Have a more romantic holiday this summer with the
Mills & Boon holiday pack.

Four brand new titles, attractively packaged for only £4.40.

The holiday pack is published on the 14th June. Look out for it
where you buy Mills & Boon.

The Rose of Romance

4 Doctor Nurse Romances
FREE

Coping with the daily tragedies and ordeals of a busy hospital, and sharing the satisfaction of a difficult job well done, people find themselves unexpectedly drawn together. Mills & Boon Doctor Nurse Romances capture perfectly the excitement, the intrigue and the emotions of modern medicine, that so often lead to overwhelming and blissful love. By becoming a regular reader of Mills & Boon Doctor Nurse Romances you can enjoy SIX superb new titles every two months plus a whole range of special benefits: your very own personal membership card, a free newsletter packed with recipes, competitions, bargain book offers, plus big cash savings.

**AND an Introductory FREE GIFT for YOU.
Turn over the page for details.**

**Fill in and send this coupon back today
and we'll send you
4 Introductory
Doctor Nurse Romances yours to keep**

FREE

At the same time we will reserve a
subscription to Mills & Boon
Doctor Nurse Romances for you. Every
two months you will receive the latest
6 new titles, delivered direct to your door.
You don't pay extra for delivery. Postage and
packing is always completely Free.
There is no obligation or commitment –
you receive books only for
as long as you want to.

**It's easy! Fill in the coupon below and return it to
MILLS & BOON READER SERVICE, FREEPOST, P.O. BOX 236,
CROYDON, SURREY CR9 9EL.**

**Please note: READERS IN SOUTH AFRICA write to
Mills & Boon Ltd., Postbag X3010,
Randburg 2125, S. Africa.**

FREE BOOKS CERTIFICATE

**To: Mills & Boon Reader Service, FREEPOST, P.O. Box 236,
Croydon, Surrey CR9 9EL.**

Please send me, free and without obligation, four Dr. Nurse Romances, and reserve a Reader
Service Subscription for me. If I decide to subscribe I shall receive, following my free parcel of
books, six new Dr. Nurse Romances every two months for £6.00*, post and packing free. If I
decide not to subscribe, I shall write to you within 10 days. The free books are mine to keep in
any case. I understand that I may cancel my subscription at any time simply by writing to you. I
am over 18 years of age.
Please write in BLOCK CAPITALS.

Name _____

Address _____

_____

_____ Postcode _____

SEND NO MONEY — TAKE NO RISKS

Remember, postcodes speed delivery. Offer applies in UK only and is not valid to present subscribers. Mills &
Boon reserve the right to exercise discretion in granting membership. If price changes are
8DN necessary you will be notified. Offer expires 31st December 1985.

EP15

* Subject to possible V.A.T.